PROTECTIVE *heart*

BRIGHTON WALSH

COPYRIGHT

For everyone who's wished their book boyfriends would walk off the page and do filthy things to them, Beck's for you.

CHAPTER ONE

BECK

PEOPLING WAS BULLSHIT, plain and simple.

Even after growing up in Starlight Cove and spending the majority of my life in a crowd, I still wasn't comfortable in one. Sometimes I just wanted to be left the fuck alone, which was damn near impossible when you had five siblings—including a twin—and lived in a modern-day Mayberry.

Starlight Cove was small, just a tiny pocket along the Maine coast with a picturesque downtown to one side and a lush crown of forest on the other. Everyone knew everyone, everyone was in everyone's business, and no one could have a moment's peace. I loved the community aspect of our little town—everyone coming together when someone was in need—but I did not love the people aspect. And there were a fuck-ton of people at the monthly Movies in the Park event, buzzing around me like flies.

Thankfully, my less than welcoming demeanor was well known in my hometown, and since I provided the best coffee in a fifty-mile radius and the best blueberry scones, well, anywhere, people tended to give me a wide berth so they could stay on my good side.

Ironically, the one person I liked outside my family hadn't known those rules when she'd moved here and had been a persistent early morning irritant from Day One. Everly Bowman was too goddamn sunshiney for anyone to have to deal with at 7 a.m., but somehow she'd gotten under my skin by showing up every day, without fail, and talking my ear off whether I'd wanted her to or not. I'd grown to tolerate her, and then accept her, and then, miraculously, started to like her.

And then I'd gone and done something even worse...

Blankets and chairs were spread across the vast lawn of the park just off Main Street. A cartoon played on the inflatable screen to keep the kids occupied as everyone found their spots and settled in for the double feature. Concession stands dotted the perimeter, but I never bought anything from them. Why would I? I cooked for a living and could make anything they had twice as good for half as much.

Besides, they didn't sell Nanaimo bars here, or anywhere around here for that matter.

"What'd you bring me?" My twin, Ford, dropped down next to me on the ground and reached for the cooler at my side.

I might've shared a womb with him, but I had no intention of sharing this, so I swatted away his questing fingers before he could touch it. "Absolutely nothing."

"No? Who's that for, then?" He held up his hand and said, "Wait, wait, let me guess... Everly's on her way."

I grunted in the affirmative but otherwise didn't respond. When he didn't have a quippy comeback, I glanced his way to find his smug-ass face already turned toward me.

"What?"

He shrugged, that smirk mocking me. "Nothing."

"It's not nothing. If it were nothing, you wouldn't have that stupid look on your face."

"I just think it's interesting, is all."

"How much you manage to irritate me every day? I wouldn't exactly call that interesting, but maybe you need to get out a bit more."

He barked out a laugh, and my lips twitched. I was closer to him than nearly anyone else in the world, but we couldn't be more opposite. Where I loathed people, Ford gravitated toward them. Especially of the female variety. He got out—and in, and out again—plenty. Definitely more than I had over the past two years, though that wasn't difficult, considering my bar was set at zero.

"What I think is interesting is how much you can't see what's right in front of you," he said.

"Your ugly face is right in front of me."

"We're twins."

"Fraternal," I said, though that didn't mean much. The McKenzie genes were strong, and all four of my brothers and I bore a striking resemblance to one another. Even our baby sister fit right in with the group, though she hadn't been blessed with the height and had maxed out almost a foot shorter than the rest of us.

"What I *meant*," he said, "was that Everly is right in front of you."

I snapped my head up and darted my gaze around, looking for the bubbly, too-bright-for-her-own-good redhead who'd somehow, beyond all reason, become my closest friend. "Where?"

Ford laughed loud enough to draw everyone's attention —exactly what I didn't want—and I showed him just how much I appreciated it with a swift elbow to his gut.

He huffed out a breath and then stood before I could land another. "Exactly," he said with a grin as he walked backward before disappearing into the crowd.

By now, I was used to the not-so-subtle hints that came from absolutely everyone. After two years of being friends with Everly, I'd been on the receiving end of the assumptions. My siblings hadn't ever hidden the fact that they thought she and I should be a couple. Everyone in the whole damn town seemed to think that. Well, everyone except the two people involved in the supposed coupling.

She was gorgeous, yes, and she was funny and smart and kind to a fault. The perfect woman, I was pretty sure. But she was...Everly. And Everly wasn't meant to be mine.

Then, as if I'd summoned her, she strode toward me across the lawn, the sun setting at her back and lighting her hair on fire. Heads turned as she walked past, people waving or stopping her to chat—something they never would've dared try with me. I didn't even think she realized how people gravitated toward her. But that made sense. All living things longed for the sun, and Everly was sunshine personified.

She dropped into the spot Ford had vacated, her brows raised, those ice-blue eyes locked on me. "Do you find it weird that couples rarely discuss butt stuff before someone shoves something up an asshole? I mean...in my world, that would merit at least a mention."

I inhaled sharply, choking on my own spit and then proceeding to hack for a full minute. When I finally had myself under control, I said, "Jesus, Everly. That's how we're starting conversations now?"

She shrugged, her eyes dancing. "Tell me I'm wrong. Tell me you'd be totally fine with a woman going to town on you and then—oop—finger in your ass."

I scrubbed a hand down my face. "Can we maybe not have our book club discussion when little Susie is five yards away?"

The last thing I needed was to discuss this week's book —which was a bit darker than her usual taste—and get hard for everyone in the damn town to see.

She tilted her head to the side to study me. "I guess. But only because you have your grumbly face on."

Her red hair was pulled back in a ponytail, her face clear of makeup except for the shit she put on her lips that made them shiny and smell like strawberries. Would they taste like strawberries, too?

I jerked my gaze away from her mouth and focused on the cartoon playing on the screen. "Grumbly is a noise, not a look."

"Oh, believe me, you've made it a look." She blew out a long sigh. "And fine, point taken. We can discuss Chapter Twenty-Two later, but I have *thoughts*."

I forced myself to stay still and pretend like I was trying to recall what happened in Chapter Twenty-Two. But I *knew* Chapter Twenty-Two. I remembered exactly what happened, and let's just say I suddenly had a newfound interest in rope play. And if past discussions were anything to go by, she'd tell me, in great detail, what she liked and didn't like about it.

Whether I'd intended to or not, I'd amassed an encyclopedia titled *Everly's Sexual Pleasure Buttons*, and each week, I added more entries. If not directly from her mouth, then from the dog-eared, highlighted, flagged sections on her physical copies. And there I'd sit, stone-faced, and pretend like I didn't want to do every goddamn one of those things to her.

Recalling how that book's hero toyed with the heroine, blindfolding her and tying her up while alternating between using a dildo and his cock had mine stiffening in my jeans. From the way Everly was shifting next to me, she, apparently, was having the same reaction. My dick throbbed as if in reminder that it'd been too damn long—two years, to be exact—since it'd had someone else besides my right hand show it some love.

Very much needing my mind focused on something else, I asked, "Where's Chuck?"

"Who?" she asked, just to be a brat.

"Your dog," I said flatly.

She smiled at me. "You know that's not her name."

I pressed my lips into a flat line. "Well, it should be. I don't know why you'd name your dog something so stupid anyway."

Her grin only widened, and I blew out a frustrated breath.

"Fine. Where's...Chuckanut?" I grumbled, forcing the name out.

She laughed, her eyes dancing, and truth be told, if my saying that made her react like that, it wasn't the worst thing in the world. "See? That wasn't so hard, was it?" She leaned in, bumping her shoulder into mine. "She's at home. Didn't feel like coming tonight. And I named her that because it reminds me of home, and it makes me happy."

"I'm pretty sure everything makes you happy."

"Not everything, but your cooking definitely does." She reached for the cooler I'd brought, and I let her—I'd learned long ago there was no use putting up any roadblocks with her after she set her mind on something. And considering it was eight o'clock at night and I'd bet my left nut she hadn't eaten much of anything today, she most definitely had her mind set on food.

She gasped, her eyes flying to mine, the smile that was bright enough to light up the night sky pointed directly at me, setting off a warm ache in my chest. "You brought me Nanaimo bars?"

"Don't I always?" I said, ignoring the pleasant little buzz that settled over me at her happiness.

"Well...yes." She lifted a single shoulder as she pulled out a bar and hummed as she made googly eyes at her favorite treat. "But I never expect it."

She moaned at her first bite, and I ignored how the sound made my cock swell in my jeans. I'd had years of practice ignoring my body's reactions to her, so it was easy to shove it down where it belonged. Namely, nowhere near Everly.

"We've been doing this for two years," I said. "You can probably stop acting surprised by now."

"But I *am* surprised," she said around a mouthful, and even that was sexy—how she pursed her lips, bringing a hand up to cover her mouth, eyes alight with pleasure. Pleasure derived directly from something *I* made for her. "I wonder if you'll bring any. I *hope* you'll bring some. But I never expect them. Ergo, pleasantly surprised."

"Your favorite pastime."

"Well, we can't all survive off surliness and pessimism."

"I prefer to call it realism, sunshine."

"And *I* prefer to call it your grumbly attitude." She rested back against the portable lounger I'd bought a while ago when these events had become a regular occurrence with us, her legs outstretched and crossed at the ankles, her flip-flops flopping as she wiggled her toes. She'd changed her toenail polish again—lime green instead of the pale purple it'd been on Tuesday. "What's playing tonight? I haven't even had time to check."

I exhaled a sharp breath and shot her a scowl because I knew exactly what that meant. "You didn't have time to eat today, either, did you?"

She cringed but tried to hide it, suddenly becoming very interested in her bar.

This fucking girl. She was driven unlike anyone I'd ever met and had a tendency to allow the rest of the world to fall away when she was working. That was great for the animals she cared for every day as the sole veterinarian in Starlight Cove, but it was bad for everything else that tended to be neglected. Like herself.

She lifted a shoulder but wouldn't meet my eyes. "I had some food."

"Some food, my ass," I grumbled, tugging my backward baseball hat off and running a frustrated hand through my hair before putting it right back on. "A fucking granola bar doesn't count."

"Uh-oh," she said. "Grumbly face *and* a hand through your hair—a sure sign you're totally fed up. Is this the night you finally kick me to the curb?"

"Would it matter if I did?"

She laughed and bumped her shoulder into mine. "Not even a little. I'd see you bright and early tomorrow morning."

She meant that, too. She'd been steadfast in that since moving here. Had proven her friendship and loyalty over and over again, which was hard won from me. After my history with— Well, after my history, I didn't like to get used to people sticking around. Didn't even let them close enough to try.

And then Everly had shoved her way in anyway.

"You can't keep doing this," I said. "What would you do if Saul told you he hasn't been feeding his dog all day?"

She gasped, gaze flying to mine. "That's awful. I'd tell him—"

"To feed his fucking dog."

Her lips twitched, so she pursed them to the side, no doubt to stop a full-blown smile from erupting. "Are you saying I'm the fucking dog in this situation?"

"You know what I mean," I grumbled.

Luckily, this wasn't my first rodeo when it came to Everly, and I'd planned for this. I reached for the second bag I'd brought as backup and dug around until I found what I wanted. Without glancing in her direction, I handed her this week's salad special.

She gasped and snatched it from me. "A spinach and strawberry salad just for me? You know, everyone in town talks about what a grouch you are, but this proves you've got a heart. Or is it just me you love?"

Something sharp tugged in my chest, and I beat it down, same as I'd been doing for the past two years. "I just don't want you to starve. I'd hardly call that love."

She bumped her knee into mine and grinned as she tucked into her meal—probably her first real one of the day. I was going to have to start making her breakfast when she stopped by the diner every morning for coffee. Straight caffeine wasn't going to cut it anymore—not when she was pulling twelve-hour days without taking a break. She'd been loving those heirloom tomatoes I'd been picking up at the farmers market. Maybe I could turn my latest omelet into a wrap, so it'd be easy and portable for her. No excuses since she could eat on the go. Then she'd—

"Is Ford here?" she asked, and she might as well have dumped a bucket of ice water over me.

I slid my gaze to her. My brother had no doubt already found a dark corner and a willing woman to occupy his time. But also, why the fuck did she want to know if he was here? "He was around a while ago. Why?"

She shrugged and speared another strawberry—she always ate them first—before popping it into her mouth. "I wanted to hire him to take care of a few things around my house."

I had a good poker face. Growing up in the family I did, getting into the shit we had, it'd been a necessity. But I was sure every ounce of irritation I felt over that inconsequential comment was currently written across my face.

Why the hell would she need to ask my brother for anything when I was sitting right next to her and perfectly fucking capable of doing it myself? My twin might've been the resort handyman and all-around town fixer-upper, but I had a toolbox. I could do things. And if I couldn't, that was what YouTube was for. If anyone was playing handyman for Everly, it sure as shit was going to be me.

"What kinds of things?" I asked.

"Oh, nothing big. Just my garbage disposal is making a really weird noise, and the dishwasher won't latch, which means I can't run it. I'm sure it's a simple fix, but you know I'm never going to get around to it."

"Considering you can barely get around to eating, no, probably not," I said dryly.

She laughed and leaned against me, nudging my shoulder until I finally lifted my arm to allow her to burrow into my side. She shimmied in with a sigh. "Much better."

This casual affection from her had taken some getting used to—my brothers weren't exactly touchy-feely, and my sister would just as soon wrap her hands around our throats as she would her arms around us for a hug—but after years of friendship, I'd grown to expect it from Everly.

Grown to crave it, too.

"I mean, I'm grateful Aunt Shirley gave me this place when she died," Everly said, "but it's not exactly in tip-top shape, you know? I don't need anything fancy, but I draw the line at doing my own dishes." She balanced her salad on her lap before pulling out her phone and navigating to her messages.

I glanced down at the screen and saw a text thread at the top from someone named Sebastian. The preview read, *See you tomorrow.*

Every muscle in my body tightened. Who the fuck was Sebastian, why the fuck did he have her number, and what the fuck was he doing with her tomorrow?

"What're you doing?" I asked, but I couldn't keep the bark out of my tone.

She raised a brow but didn't look in my direction. "I know, no cell phones during the movies. Sorry, sorry. But I'll forget if I don't send Ford a text right now. I just want to see if he has time this week to—"

I reached over, snatched the phone from her hands, and slid it into my pocket.

"Hey!" She huffed, elbowing me in the side, so I grabbed that, too, and pulled her even closer, caging her against me. "I was almost done."

"Don't bother. Addison's been keeping him pretty busy at the resort." Not exactly a lie, considering our baby sister was a dictator when it came to bossing her brothers around. "But I'll swing by your place and see what I can do."

Correction—I'd take care of it, whatever it was, and she wouldn't have to worry about it at all.

She rested her hand on my chest as she shot me her thousand-watt smile, and something tugged low in my gut. A tug I batted away easily since I'd been doing so for two years. Everly wasn't interested in a relationship, and she'd said as much when she'd broken up with that tool she'd been dating when she'd first moved here.

Besides that, I couldn't go there with her. I didn't make friends easily—or at all—and other than my family, Everly was it for me. I refused to screw that up. Not when I had a one hundred percent fail rate for every past relationship I'd ever had, dating all the way back to Jackie Henderson in the sixth grade.

Everly was too important to me to take a chance on something that would, without a doubt, crash and burn.

CHAPTER TWO

EVERLY

MOVING to Starlight Cove hadn't been in my five-year plan. Or my ten-year plan. Or my life plan, period, actually. While I'd spent every summer break of my childhood here with my aunt—Starlight Cove's own Dr. Doolittle—being her shadow as she cared for every animal within seventy-five miles, uprooting my entire life to a tiny dot on the map three thousand miles away from home hadn't been on my radar.

But then she'd died two years ago—not unexpectedly, thanks to a CT scan that had showed cancer almost three years before she'd passed—and bequeathed me her home and attached vet clinic—completely unexpectedly, thanks to the fact that I technically wasn't even a Bowman. Aunt Shirley had been my dad's only sibling and hadn't had any children of her own, but still...I hadn't expected this. None of us had.

Yes, I'd studied veterinary medicine, and it'd been my plan to become a vet since I was ten years old and had witnessed my first calf birth right here in Starlight Cove. And yes, Aunt Shirley had taken me under her wing and shown me the ropes before I'd even realized this was what I wanted to do with my life. But the fact of the matter was, I was a Bowman in name only. Even though my younger brother had zero interest in caring for animals and preferred to spend his time with numbers, *he* was a Bowman by blood.

That I was adopted had never been a secret. Neither had the fact that my infertile—or so they thought—parents had miraculously conceived my baby brother just a few months after adopting me. I was their angel, and he was their miracle—that was what they always said. They'd never once made me feel like an outsider, despite our differences as apparent as a billboard. Being the only short, blue-eyed redhead in a family of people the tall, dark, and handsome moniker was based on led to a whole lot of mailman jokes that I hadn't made heads or tails of when I was younger but had sunk in, nonetheless.

My family may not ever have tried to make me feel like an outsider, but I had that covered all on my own, and I'd spent my life overcompensating for the fact that I didn't always feel like I belonged.

So now, despite that Starlight Cove hadn't been in my plans, there'd been no way I'd turn my nose up at the gift my aunt could've given anyone else. Plus, it'd been an adventure—a sometimes rocky adventure, but an adventure, regardless. I loved meeting new people, making new friends, immersing myself in new surroundings.

And, okay, so Starlight Cove and I hadn't quite settled into a rhythm yet. After two years, I still felt like an outsider most days—fine, *every* day—but it wasn't all bad. I'd found one safe space in this new life.

I snuggled into the warmth of Beck's side, one of my few comforts in this town, and stared blankly at the inflatable screen showing the first movie of the double feature. As much as I tried, movies rarely held my focus—my brain was always going a million miles an hour, and nothing seemed to keep it from doing so. Not meditation, not music, not brain exercises...nada. Which meant I had to ask Beck every fifteen minutes what was going on. My grumbly bestie just *loved* that.

"Do we know who that guy is and why he's there?" I whispered around a mouthful of Nanaimo bar as I pointed to the man in the corner of the screen.

Beck slid his eyes to me, the irritation plain on his face, even under the cloak of darkness. "They *just* explained who he is and why he's there. Fuck, sunshine, you drive me crazy."

"Can't help it."

"I think it's more than that. I think you do it on purpose."

"I do not."

"No? Every week, it's the same damn thing. What goes through that pretty head of yours while you're supposed to be watching these movies?"

I shrugged. "Pretty much everything. My schedule for tomorrow, any animals who were sent home for post-op recovery, what food I have in my fridge, when I'm ever going to be able to go grocery shopping, the three unread text messages on my phone, how I can—"

"All right. Jesus. I get it. Does your brain ever turn off?"

"Never." And I really meant *never*, but I wouldn't mention to him that my nonstop brain interfered with sex, too. Which was why it took my own diligence and favorite clit-sucking godsend of a toy to get me off. Beck and I were close—hell, we even read spicy books together that talked about, in explicit detail, using said toy—but telling him how I masturbated felt like a step too far.

He blew out a frustrated breath, his mouth set in a flat line, and I hit him with the full force of what he called my Everly Voodoo. Big eyes, bright smile, and a hopeful expression he couldn't say no to—or if he could, I hadn't yet encountered such a situation.

"Why the hell do we even come to these?" he grumbled more to himself than to me.

"Because you love hanging out with me."

He grunted in response, but I knew he enjoyed our time together as much as I did. Beck was all tough exterior with a gooey marshmallow center—something he didn't let anyone but me see—and even that was only because I looked really damn hard. It may have taken months of persistence on my part, but I'd finally broken him down. Hell, even his nickname for me had changed in that time. Not *literally*—he'd called me sunshine since the first day I'd popped into the diner seeking caffeine after my morning run—but where it had once been laced with scorn and irritation, now it held an underlying fondness I knew he would deny to his dying breath.

"Fine," he said with a sigh, and I grinned up at him. "That guy"—he pointed to the man in question—"is the bad guy, but he's got everyone else fooled. And if you don't shut up and watch, you're going to miss the best part."

I gasped. "You've already seen this?"

"Of course. Like I could handle watching a movie with you for the first time. I'd never hear anything over your incessant questions and comments."

"Oh, come on. I'm not that bad. It'd be great."

"It'd be aneurysm-inducing."

I laughed, clapping a hand over my mouth when a few people shot their gazes our way. I lowered my voice and leaned into him, my lips close to his ear. "You're so sweet to me."

He shifted in his seat, then with the hand draped over my shoulders, he tugged on my ponytail but otherwise didn't say a word. But he didn't have to. I snuggled into him, settling into the warmth of his side and breathing in the familiar scent that had come to feel like home.

It was exactly this companionship we had that had made my transition to Starlight Cove easy. Or easier, at least.

And I wouldn't change it for the world.

CHAPTER THREE

BECK

THE NEXT EVENING, I flipped the sign hanging in the front window of the diner to *Closed* and locked the door. My sister, Addison, sat at the counter, laptop open in front of her, with her tablet set up, all while she typed rapidly on her phone. I could honestly say I had no idea what she did for the resort—her title of social media manager and resort liaison meant fuck all to me—only that she was always busy and never without technology at her fingertips as she attempted to right the sinking ship that was this resort. Against all odds, she'd partially succeeded, too. But I was old enough to remember exactly how bad it could get. Old enough, too, to know those peaks never lasted.

"I'm leaving, so that means lights off." I strode past her and grabbed my toolbox from behind the counter.

Without looking up, she waved a hand in the air. "Leave them. I'll take care of it. Where're you headed?"

"Swinging by Everly's."

She snapped her head up, her eyes glittering with interest. "Oh, *really*."

Jesus Christ. She acted like Everly and I were having a secret affair instead of one friend doing something for the other. I refused to give Addison a reaction since goading me about Everly was one of her favorite things to do.

"Her garbage disposal isn't working, and her dishwasher won't close. She was trying to hire Ford to do it for her, so I told her I'd handle it. She doesn't need to waste her money when I'm perfectly capable."

"Perfectly capable or positively *dying* to take care of it for her?"

I grunted but otherwise didn't respond. So what if I enjoyed making sure she had what she needed? That was what friends did.

"I'm just saying…" Addison turned her attention back to one of her three screens. "You're not fooling anybody but yourself, buddy."

This time, I couldn't keep the eye roll to myself as I strolled out the back door without another word. It was late enough that darkness had fallen, the stars twinkling in the sky as the ocean lapped at the shore a hundred yards away. Some days, it sucked living above the diner—and this close to my siblings—but having the Atlantic Ocean as my backyard never did.

On my way to my truck, I thumbed out a text to Everly to see if she was home. It didn't matter if she was or not. I could let myself in with my key, fix what needed fixing, and be gone before she even knew I was there.

8:52 p.m.
You home?

The dots didn't immediately pop up, so I placed my toolbox in the truck bed and climbed into the cab. I'd just turned my key in the ignition when my phone buzzed with a text.

8:53 p.m.
Not exactly. I'm at the clinic. Mrs. Farmington's dog decided he was very hungry for socks today. Gonna be here a while. What's up?

8:53 p.m.
Nothing. Do your thing.

Then, I added:

8:54 p.m.
And text me after you get home and actually lock your doors.

I tossed my phone in the passenger's seat and headed toward town and to Everly's place. Either she'd see my truck in her driveway since the clinic was attached to her house, or she'd come home and find all her shit fixed and know I'd been there.

I pulled into the driveway of the tri-level home, the single story of which served as the clinic. After grabbing my toolbox out of the truck bed, I strolled up to the back door. The light in the kitchen was on, but that didn't mean anything. Whenever there was an emergency, she left in a flurry with little thought. I'd gotten many a text as she was heading into surgery, asking me to turn off her curling iron or to check to see if her gas stove was still on or to blow out a candle she'd left burning. She was going to give me a goddamn heart attack one of these days. She also rarely remembered to lock her door, which I'd snapped at her about more than once. I didn't care if our crime rate was comically low. It wasn't *none*.

I tried the knob, anticipating the worst but, thankfully, found it locked. Usually, the sound of keys was enough for her dog to absolutely lose her shit and come running, so I was surprised and a little on guard when I let myself in to no greeting—exuberant or otherwise. Everly didn't usually bring Chuck over to the clinic when she performed surgeries, but maybe she'd made an exception tonight.

I closed the door behind me and set my toolbox on the counter, checking first to make sure the stove was off— check—before scanning the place for anything out of the ordinary. My gaze automatically bypassed the person sitting at her kitchen table before snapping back, and my shoulders stiffened.

A man around my age stared back at me, brows raised, wearing nothing but a pair of goddamn basketball shorts, his dark brown hair wet like he'd just gotten out of the shower.

"Who the fuck are you?" I barked, glancing around to make sure Everly wasn't here and in trouble, never mind that her text had just confirmed she was at the clinic. When it came to her, I wasn't always known for thinking rationally.

I'd lived in Starlight Cove my entire life, and thus I knew each and every resident within. Knew their families, too, and their friends, and their friends' friends. And running the diner meant I knew even those strays who didn't reside here but just stepped foot in our little town, and I'd never seen this fucker before a day in my life.

With a spoonful of cereal halfway to his mouth, Fucker gave me a once-over, quickly disregarding my backward baseball hat, plain gray T-shirt, and worn jeans. "I'm Sebastian. Who the fuck are you?"

Sebastian, Sebastian... Why did I recognize that—

I narrowed my eyes on him. That'd been the name I'd seen on Everly's texts last night. Before yesterday, I hadn't heard a single thing about this guy, and now suddenly, *Sebastian* was texting her and hanging out in her home while she wasn't there, showering, and eating a bowl of cereal like he owned the damn place? "How'd you get in here?"

"Everly, obviously." Then, under his breath, he said, "They don't grow 'em smart around here, do they?"

"What the fuck did you just say?"

"I said," he enunciated, louder than necessary, "how'd *you* get in?"

"My key." I pulled my ring from my pocket and held it up. That's right. I had a key to her place. One I used enough that I'd just added it to my own set. What'd he think of that?

He glanced to the toolbox on the counter, then regarded me with raised brows. "I didn't realize she gave the handyman free entrance to her home."

I clenched my jaw, irritation getting the better of me. "I'm not the *handyman*. I'm her—" I cut myself off, for some reason not wanting to admit to this cockmuppet that I was just her friend. So instead, I settled on another truth. "I'm the guy she calls when she needs help."

I didn't know who the fuck this guy was, why he was in Everly's home at nine o'clock at night—okay, so I could guess on that one, but I shoved the thought out of my mind as quickly as it came—or why he wasn't able to take care of the shit that needed fixing, only that *I* was the one who'd shown up for her how she needed.

It was late—way too late for a casual date, especially when Everly was currently at the clinic side of the house, taking care of a sock-eater. This guy could use her shower, eat her food, and—probably—sleep in her bed, but he couldn't be bothered to fix her disposal or dishwasher?

That was real fucking nice. What the hell kind of men was she involved with?

Thankfully, I'd never had the misfortune of meeting anyone she'd been dating. When she'd moved here, she'd been in a long-distance relationship with someone—James...Justin...Jonah... Something that began with a J, so I'd just started calling him Jackass. Their relationship had lasted all of three months before she'd called it quits and declared a self-imposed man embargo while she'd gotten acclimated to Starlight Cove and the brand-new clinic, following her aunt's passing.

A self-imposed man embargo that I was *totally* on board with. God knew how I'd handle seeing her dating anyone in town.

But even though I'd never met anyone she'd been involved with, I'd had plenty of chances to imagine what they'd be like. I figured she'd go for someone who'd challenge her and make her laugh. Definitely well educated, but he wouldn't be pompous about it because she'd hate that—this guy struck out on that, at least.

"What's your name?" he asked. "You know, for the police report."

I nearly snorted. Let him call. I'd love to have my eldest brother and town sheriff dragged out for some bullshit report. Brady would just love that. "Great. Tell them Beck says hi."

His brows lifted even farther, and he gave me another

once-over, cocking his head to the side like he couldn't quite work out a puzzle. "So, you're Beck."

He'd heard of me? Good. From his tone, he obviously wasn't a fan. Well, he better get real fucking comfortable real fucking quick with Everly's and my friendship because I wasn't going anywhere.

"As you can see, Evie's not here," he said, gesturing to the empty house.

Evie? This assclown was already on a nickname basis with her? What the fuck.

"I know. She told me." *Yeah, we talk and she gave me a key and I'm the guy she comes to when she needs something and I have my own nickname for her, too, so good luck, pal.* "Where's Chuckanut?"

Sylvester—or whatever the fuck his name was—wrinkled his nose. "Brought him with her. Dogs and I don't get along."

I didn't trust someone who didn't like dogs. And considering Everly's entire life revolved around animals, those two weren't off to a great start. What the hell did she see in this guy?

"Now that we've established neither Evie nor her dog are here, can I help you with something?"

"Nope." I turned my back on him and opened my tool-box, riffling through for what I needed. "Don't mind me while I do your job for you."

"Excuse me?"

I glanced at him over my shoulder and lifted my chin

toward the dishwasher. "Didn't you notice this was broken?"

"Of course I noticed it was broken." He rolled his eyes as he shoveled another spoonful of cereal into his mouth. "I'm not an idiot."

"Could've fooled me," I said under my breath.

"What was that?"

"I said, you noticed it was broken, and yet you're not over here fixing it. *I* am."

He scoffed. "It's not like I have tools here, man."

And grabbing them from his place was, what? Too much of an inconvenience for this guy? Couldn't be bothered to help out the woman he was, apparently, in some sort of relationship with? Fuck, he really was a shitbag.

"All I know is Everly's mentioned this a couple times" —okay, so it was once, just the night before, but Stuart didn't need to know that—"which means either you don't listen when she talks, or she tells me more than you." I shrugged like I didn't care either way.

He snorted and propped his definitely smaller-than-mine arms on the table and raised a brow. "You don't want to get into the *who knows Evie better* game, I can promise you that."

I set my toolbox on the floor in front of the sink, turned around, and leaned back against the counter, arms crossed over my chest. This was going to be fun. "Oh yeah? Try me."

He laughed then, a pompous, arrogant sound that set

my teeth on edge. Where the fuck did she find this guy? Pottery Barn? "Fine, let's start easy. Her favorite movie is *The Notebook*."

I rolled my eyes. This guy wasn't even trying. "That's what she *pretends* her favorite movie is, but it's really *Bridesmaids*."

Simon's brows drew down, and he straightened a bit more in his chair, as if finally realizing this was a competition. And I was winning. "She's a weirdo who loves brussels sprouts."

"Actually, she hates brussels sprouts. Or she did until I roasted them for her with bacon and Parmesan cheese."

His scowl deepened. "Her favorite book is *Pride & Prejudice*."

I snorted. Jesus, did this guy know her at all, or was he just there to get in her pants? "Maybe in high school. Her tastes have...matured a bit." That was an understatement, considering the book we were reading this week dabbled in bondage and some light breath play—not that I minded.

Okay, I minded a little. I'd had more blue balls since beginning our unofficial book club over the winter than I'd had since I was a teenager. But most midafternoons at the diner were boring as hell—especially prior to the increased business we'd been having the past couple weeks—and those books filled my time. And my jeans.

"Oh yeah?" Samuel asked. "What's it now?"

Yeah, like I was going to help this guy figure out what

turned Everly on. He was on his own. "Why the hell should I tell you?"

He lifted his brows and held up a hand. "Hey, man. This was your idea. Fine by me if you want to forfeit."

My not answering his questions didn't mean I was forfeiting. Only someone completely delusional would think they knew her better since they could recite the things she'd loved ten or more years ago. But there was no denying I knew her better *now*.

No denying he knew her better then, either. Was this jackass someone from her past? That would explain the obvious comfort he had here...everything he knew about her...the nickname...

Everly was a serial monogamist who'd had three long-term boyfriends in her life—high school, college, and during her veterinary program. There was no way this was Jackass whom she'd been dating when she moved here. But... Fuck. Hadn't high school guy's name started with an S?

I didn't respond to him and instead focused on the task at hand, all the while stewing over who this guy was and what the hell he was doing back in her life.

More importantly, why hadn't she told me anything about him? She hadn't mentioned that she was seeing someone...not even that she'd decided she was ready to date again.

Though from the apparent assmonkey this guy was, that wasn't so surprising. She was probably embarrassed to mention him because she knew I'd make sure he was a good guy before giving my stamp of approval.

Okay, there'd be no stamp of approval. I'd hate every single man she brought by, even if he was a member of the Peace Corps and spent his days saving kittens from trees.

Everly was the kind of woman to be worshipped. She deserved someone who'd treat her right. Someone who'd happily give her everything she needed, just to see her smile.

And there was no fucking way it was this guy.

CHAPTER FOUR

BECK

SIX-THIRTY IN THE morning was too fucking early to deal with my siblings. Especially after I'd spent last night in a pissing match with some fuck-head Everly hadn't even mentioned in passing.

I'd worked on her dishwasher and disposal for about forty-five minutes, all while the shirtless asshat had looked on, not offering to raise a finger as he ate his cereal and fucked around on his phone. And then, when I'd finished up everything she'd mentioned—and even fixed a few things she hadn't—I'd left him in her house while I'd returned to mine, hating every second of it.

He wasn't a good fit for her, but I didn't know how to tell her that. It wasn't something we'd had to navigate in our friendship, but there was no way I'd be able to sit silently by while she kept seeing that cheesedick.

Doing as I'd asked, she'd texted just after 1 a.m. that

she was safely behind her locked door and the sock-hungry dog was recovering comfortably.

It hadn't been the right time to ask about Seth. To grill her on who the fuck the guy was taking up residence in her home like he owned the place. But it'd been swirling around in my head since I'd left her house, and I couldn't seem to think of anything but that.

For once, my sister had agreed to hold the morning meeting in the diner—the resort's recent brush with success seemed to have softened her slightly—and my siblings, save for Brady, gathered around the space. I'd been asking for this location switch for months. It only made sense to hold these meetings here instead of the main inn because... Well, because it was a hell of a lot more convenient for me since I lived just upstairs and since I was the only one who had to be somewhere on a schedule—7:00 on the dot—no matter how long Addison insisted on running her mouth. Never mind that Everly was the only person who'd notice if I was a few minutes late. My siblings didn't need to know that.

Hoping to make this a permanent switch and not above bribery, I'd pulled out all the stops. The counter was covered with a huge spread, even though my brother Aiden—keeper of the resort and the budget—would prob-ably have my ass for it. I'd needed to keep my mind busy last night after I'd gotten back from Everly's and waited for her *all good* text, anyway, and nothing kept my mind occu-pied like spending time in the kitchen. I'd had a temper growing up and had been in too many fights to count. It was after one that'd landed me an in-school suspension for a week that my mom had guided me to cooking, and it'd stuck.

So, while stewing over Spencer lounging in Everly's home while she wasn't there—worse, while she *was*—I'd spent a couple hours preparing muffins, banana bread, coffee cake, and blueberry scones. And from how my siblings had descended on the spread like a pack of wolves when they'd first stepped foot in the diner, I'd say they were going over pretty well.

Levi—youngest McKenzie boy and all-around recluse —sat in a corner all by himself, his brows drawn in a scowl, though I had no idea why. The lucky bastard had managed to get Addison to agree that he only needed to attend one of these stupid meetings per month.

She and Aiden sat at a table dead center, both ignoring each other and everyone else as they ate their baked goods, their attentions locked on their phones. And Ford sat at the counter on one of the barstools, his eyes bleary, no doubt thanks to another late night.

"Hit me," he said, knocking twice on the counter, and I grabbed a mug before pouring him a cup of coffee. "Was last night the night?"

"The night for what?"

"You to get your head out of your ass."

"No idea what you're talking about."

"I'll take that as a no, then."

Before I could ask what he meant, Brady, eldest McKenzie and Starlight Cove's sheriff, strolled in behind Luna, his new girlfriend—and resort savior, thanks to a viral video. She grinned at me and sat at the counter next to Ford, seemingly unconcerned by the daggers Brady was shooting at her ass and the scowl on his face as he settled on her other side.

"Let's get started, shall we?" Addison said as she clapped her hands like the drill sergeant she liked to pretend she was. "This layout's not ideal, but it will have to do."

I clenched my jaw and reminded myself I was supposed to be wooing her over to my side today. That worked for all of two seconds before I said, "How about those muffins you demolished like they owed you money? Were they ideal?"

"Mine were delicious, thanks for asking," Ford said as he licked his fingers. I hadn't even realized he'd taken one, let alone finished multiple. The guy ate like a fucking horse.

"Can we get on with this?" Levi said from his hovel in the corner. "If I have to be here, I'd like it to last as little time as possible."

The ass didn't even know how good he had it. Addison turned in his direction, no doubt ready to lay into him, but the buzzing of her phone interrupted her. Without saying a word to anyone, she shifted her attention to respond to whatever message had arrived, her thumbs flying over her phone.

Levi dropped his head back on a groan. "Jesus Christ, Addison. If all the meetings are going to be like this, I'm sending my shit in via email."

"Have a muffin and shut up," Addison said without lifting her eyes from the screen. "It's from Harper."

It was nearly comical watching my siblings' reactions to that bit of news, all of their eyes landing on Levi to witness his response to hearing Harper's name. When they'd been younger, she and Levi had been inseparable, but in the ten years since that time, something had happened between them. What, we had no idea, but it couldn't have been good. Not when their rocky history had almost cost us the featured article on the resort Harper had been assigned to write.

Sadly, though we were all waiting for it, Levi didn't react, save for the slight tightening of his jaw. His poker face was better than mine.

Aiden slid his gaze back to Addison. "They already approved the article. No take backs."

"She's not taking it back," Addison said with a roll of her eyes as she finally set her phone on the table. "She just wanted to check and see if bookings were still up thanks to Luna's TikTok debut."

Initially, I'd viewed the modern-day hippie as I did everyone else—with irritation, frustration, or indifference.

And after she proved to be a bit of a speed bump for the resort, I wasn't sure how this whole thing would shake out, considering she'd spent a good deal of time chaining herself to the tree bordering our property and getting herself arrested by her now-boyfriend. But in the few short months she'd been in Starlight Cove, she'd managed not only to snag my unsnaggable brother but also to do something we hadn't been able to for the past decade—breathe life back into this resort.

So, yeah, I'd named an omelet after her. Hell, I'd name the whole menu after her if she could keep up this momentum.

"Which, by the way, they are," Addison continued. "We're officially booked out through June. And in case anyone hasn't been paying attention, that hasn't happened in years."

"Yes, yes, it's very exciting," I said, tone flat. I uncrossed my arms and gestured to the spread laid out across the counter. "As you can see, I prepared."

"Oh, you knew this was going to happen, did you?" Addison scoffed and rolled her eyes.

"Had a feeling, yeah. I also have a feeling Luna's going to want this." I turned around to grab her morning green juice I'd made before she came in and set it in front of her. Then I turned my back on them and grabbed a to-go cup for Everly's morning coffee. "And Everly's going to be here in about thirty seconds for her daily pick-me-up."

She ran along the beach every morning, and no matter the weather, I could still set my clock by her appearance. I filled her cup three-quarters of the way with coffee and topped it with cream before adding two sugars. The hum of voices rose as everyone continued trading barbs back and forth—it was a nonstop bickerfest when the six of us were together—and I turned when the bells over the door chimed, expecting Everly to walk in, smile on her face despite how early it was or the fact that she'd just run five miles.

Instead, a guy strolled in, head down as he stared at his phone, so I couldn't see his face.

"Hey, we're not actually open yet," I said as the man turned toward me, and a cannonball landed in my gut. *Sebastian.*

Shirtless man, cereal eater, past-Everly secret keeper, and my number one enemy, considering it was ass o'clock in the morning, and Everly strolled in right behind him, which meant what I'd feared was true...

This asshole had stayed with her last night.

CHAPTER FIVE

EVERLY

I MIGHT'VE LIVED in Starlight Cove for a couple years, but this was the first time anyone in my family had visited me. Mostly, that was on me. I missed home, so whenever I had a break in my schedule—which, truth be told, was hardly ever since I was the sole vet around—I flew back to Washington.

But my little brother was here for a couple days, and I'd been so excited to show him around since he hadn't been here in fifteen years. We were off to a bit of a rocky start, though.

First, when he'd arrived at my house, he'd made a face like he was stepping into the sewer. And, yeah, that probably had more to do with the fact that he was horrifically allergic to dogs and my twenty-five-pound exuberance machine had jumped right up to welcome him to our home than it was a reflection on his surroundings, but still

Second, I'd had an emergency surgery pop up, so our planned night out in Starlight Cove had been nixed. Worse, Beck tended to spoil me in the food department—bonus points for your best friend cooking for a living—so the last time I did a full stock-up at the grocery store was...well, I couldn't remember. Which meant all I had available was my standard cuisine of cereal.

And finally, I'd hoped for some quick bonding time between my little brother and my bestie during my usual morning stop. Instead, Ash had spent the entire time we'd been in the diner with his face buried in his phone, no doubt secretly trolling his girlfriend—*ex*-girlfriend—and tormenting himself over every picture and status update, and Beck had spent it glaring daggers at anything that moved.

So, yeah. It could've gone better. But it hadn't been all bad, especially with the carb cornucopia Beck had spread out today. If I had one of his blueberry scones as my last meal, I'd die a happy woman.

"So, what'd you think of the diner?" I asked as I drove us back to my place. I wished I were running—I always felt a bit out of whack when I messed with my schedule—but my brother would rather, and I quote, shove toothpicks under his nails than run for fun. "Cute, right?"

Ash shrugged, his attention—you guessed it—on his phone. "I've eaten better. And the company left a lot to be desired."

"Hey!" I reached over and smacked him in the stomach. "Rude."

"I didn't mean *you*." He rolled his eyes. "I meant the asshole in the hat. The guy who let himself into your house last night while you were gone. We should talk about that, by the way."

I snapped my head in his direction, darting my gaze back to the road to make sure I wasn't veering off course. "Wait...Beck came by last night? When? For what?"

"While you were at the clinic."

"Huh." That must've been what his texts had been all about. But it was weird that he'd dropped by, obviously run into my brother, and then he just...hadn't said anything. Though, we hadn't exactly had a lot of time—or any, really —to chat since I'd gotten in late last night—or rather, very early this morning—and he'd already been at the resort meeting when I'd woken up. I hadn't even had a chance to let him know Ash was in town, and since Addison had cracked the whip the entire time we were in the diner, this morning wasn't the meet-and-greet I'd hoped.

"As for what," he said, "my guess is his intention was to piss a circle around your house since you were unavailable and have a dick-measuring contest, never mind that I'm your *brother*." He shuddered. "Doesn't take much to make him feel threatened, does it? I'm surprised he didn't get out a tape measure and drop trou."

I snorted. It wasn't hard to imagine Beck coming off like that to a newcomer, and he tended to be extra protective of me around other men. Apparently that bled over to my family, too. That was just part of his charm and not something he employed often, considering how few prospects I had...or even wanted.

After breaking things off with Jeremy shortly after moving here, I hadn't wanted the added pressure and stress of making a new relationship work on top of everything else. It'd already been enough of an adjustment to make the transition smooth at the clinic—not to mention my moving clear across the country. I hadn't needed to add navigating a new relationship onto my plate, too. I *didn't* need to. I was perfectly satisfied with the companionship I had in the form of a growly best friend who loved stuffing me with delicious food and offering cuddles whenever I bullied him into giving them.

I shook my head. "It's not like that with us."

"Does *he* know that?"

I rolled my eyes. "I don't know for certain, but I think he's probably aware we've never slept together, yes."

Ash shot me a blank stare—his *you are such an idiot* look that he'd perfected over his twenty-nine years. "I don't understand your brain sometimes. How are you so naive?"

I gasped. "I am *not* naive."

Okay, so my romantic life was fairly vanilla—and, like, imitation vanilla. Not even vanilla bean over here. I certainly wasn't setting records with three lovers in thirty years. But even if I hadn't lived out any adventures in real life, my ever-trusty romances broadened my horizons in ways that would've horrified my brother. And *had*, actually. When I was in college, I'd accidentally sent him a text meant for my roommate—also named Ash—that may or may not have been a link to a particularly steamy book. And I may or may not have gone into detail about which scenes I loved and why she should read.

After reaming me a new asshole, he'd demanded I either lose his number or change his contact info to his *real* name, despite the fact that I'd never called him Sebastian a day in my life.

"Fine," he conceded. "Not naive. Oblivious."

I huffed as I pulled into my driveway and shut off the car. "That's not any better."

"I'm just saying, there was something there."

"Yeah, *friendship*. You remember what that's like, right?"

As soon as the words left my mouth, I cringed, immediately wanting to snatch them back before they reached his ears. Considering he was currently escaping his recent breakup from the woman who'd started out as his best friend, that was a low blow on my part—even if unintended—and I should've known better. Maybe he was onto something with the whole oblivious thing.

"Sorry. I didn't mean—"

"Whatever. You have a point," he said. "And, yes, I remember what friendship is like. I also remember what it's like to want to fuck my friend. And Beck's there, Evie."

"No, he's not. You're totally misreading it. He barely tolerates me!" I slid the key into the back door's dead bolt, only to find I'd forgotten to lock up when we'd left. Whoops. Definitely would not be mentioning that to Beck —his grumbly face turned downright murderous when I did that. But between Chuckanut's incessant barks that would hopefully scare off any robbers and the fact that this was Starlight Cove, I wasn't too worried about intruders popping in before 8 a.m.

"What was with the cringe?" he asked.

"What? Oh, nothing. Beck just hates when I don't lock up, and I'm always forgetting. If it's not that, it's leaving my curling iron or stove on, or all my windows open when it's about to rain, or forgetting to close the gate. Just me and my obliviousness, apparently." I gripped the doorknob and turned my head toward him. "Prepare yourself."

"For wh—"

He didn't get the words out before I opened the door, and a blur of black and gray dashed toward us. Ash froze as I squatted to give my dog all kinds of love. She was one of the best things to fall into my lap since arriving in this town, and I was so grateful for her company. It didn't matter if I was gone for five minutes or five hours, she responded the same way—like my walking through the door was the best minute of her life.

Ash sidestepped Chuckanut, nose crinkling as he did so, and settled himself across the room, as far away as he could get while still in my line of vision. With his arms folded over his chest, he leaned back against the counter, ankles crossed and eyebrow raised. "So let me get this straight. Beck knows how you take your coffee and the exact minute you'll be there in the mornings, has a key to your place, lets himself in at any time for any reason, even when you're not here, so he can fix whatever you need taken care of, cooks you breakfast, lunch, and dinner, has an attitude with any other male in your life, and gets upset when you're not being safe. Have I got that about right?"

"Um..." When he laid it all out like that, it did sound a little over the top. "It's not *always* breakfast, lunch, and dinner..."

"Hate to tell you this, sis, but you're in a relationship. You're just not having sex."

"What?" I huffed out a laugh and stood, Chuckanut following on my heels. "No. We're not. We're in a *friendship* without the sex. Didn't you do things like that for Mandy before you guys hooked up?"

He raised his brows and looked at me like I was an idiot. "I don't understand how you can be so fucking smart and so fucking dumb at the same time."

I scowled and elbowed him in the gut as I passed. "Don't be a jerk, or I'll let Chuckanut sleep next to you tonight."

"I'm not trying to be a jerk. I'm trying to get you to open your eyes. And to answer your question, yes, I did things like that for Mandy before we hooked up."

"Great, so you—"

"*And then we hooked up,*" he interrupted, enunciating each word far too loudly for the small kitchen.

I shook my head. "Well, that's you. That's not us."

"That might not be you, but I'd bet good money it's him."

"Hey, I have an idea," I said with overexaggerated enthusiasm. "How about instead of microanalyzing *my* life, you figure out your own shit? I don't even know what you're doing here."

"I'm visiting my sister. Thought that was pretty obvious."

"You're acting like a troll."

"Well, excuse the fuck out of me. I just ended my six-year relationship, so I'm sorry I'm not all sunshine and rainbows."

I blew out a sigh and braced myself against the counter next to him, bumping my shoulder into his. "You don't have to be all sunshine and rainbows, but I'm just not sure what sleeping on my couch is doing for you."

"Well, I was *supposed* to have some desperately needed sister time."

"Nice try, but considering you've spent your 'desperately needed' sister time scrolling Mandy's social media on a burner account just so you can see if she's as miserable as you, I'm not buying it."

"She's not, by the way."

"You don't have to be, either, you know. You already paid for that trip to Jamaica you guys were supposed to go on, so my question is, why aren't you taking advantage of it?"

"It's an all-inclusive vacation for two."

"Double the drinks and dessert. I don't see the problem."

"It's going to suck ass. Everyone's going to look at me with sad eyes."

"Maybe." I shrugged. "Or *maybe* they'll comp you a room upgrade and a nice massage because you look so pitiful. And you do, you know. You look incredibly pitiful."

He huffed out a laugh and shook his head. "Speaking of pitiful...does she need something?" Ash pointed to Chuckanut, who sat in front of her bowl, shifting her gaze from her very empty food dish to me and back again.

"Nice try," I said to her with a laugh, "but I already fed you this morning."

As soon as the words left my mouth, she bounded off into the living room, probably to go toy hunting since her ploy hadn't worked.

I twisted to face my brother, hip resting against the counter. "Look, all I'm saying is I'd rather be wallowing in paradise than couching it with my sister while popping the max dose of Benadryl every day just so I could stay vertical."

"If you wanted to get rid of me, you could've just said so."

"I don't want to get rid of you." I gripped his forearm and gave it a shake. "I love you and want you to be happy. And I don't think that's going to happen here."

He ran a hand through his hair and sighed. "Yeah, well, that makes two of us."

"So, you'll go?"

"I wasn't talking about me. I was talking about you."

"Um...I don't have a trip to Jamaica on the books."

"I mean I want you to be happy, and I don't think you are here."

At that, I jerked back, furrowing my brow as I stared at him. "What? I am. I love Starlight Cove."

He lifted a single shoulder and stared at me with those all-knowing eyes that always managed to see through everything. "So you say. But then I get here, and your closest friend is a Grade A dickbag, your evenings are interrupted by emergency appointments, you're working so much you barely have time to breathe, let alone eat, your fridge is empty—your *home* is empty, and I'm not just talking about the food." He blew out a long breath and knocked my shoulder with his. "Me, Mom, and Dad...we're not here. Your entire support system is in Washington. Why aren't you?"

CHAPTER SIX

BECK

"THIS IS my first night in days without Addison riding my ass," I grumbled as I wiped down the last table before turning the sign to *Closed* and locking the diner door. "She won't quit."

Ford sat on a stool, elbows braced on the counter. "Tell me about it. If I don't have a shift at the firehouse, she's got me running all over the damn place. Yeah, the extra bookings at the resort are nice, but I need a fucking break. If this keeps up, we're going to have to hire some actual help that isn't us."

"So we're agreed we need to haul ass—"

"Before she finds us? Yep." He stood, grabbing his portable radio from its place on the counter. He'd been on call, which meant the low hum of mostly static from the radio had been our background noise for the evening.

As soon as we were upstairs at my place, Ford headed

straight for the fridge and pulled out a beer for himself before passing a water bottle to me. He set the radio on the table and dropped into one of my two loungers. "What's Everly been up to? Is the new guy still on the scene?"

A spike of jealousy shot through me at the mention of the asshole she'd been spending time with. I hated to think about him, and I hated my brother for bringing it up, especially when I'd been doing everything in my power to ignore it. "Don't know."

He froze with his beer halfway to his mouth, his brows lifted. "You don't know?"

"That's what I said."

"So, what, you just haven't asked?"

"No, I haven't. We've had other shit to talk about." Or, more accurately, we hadn't had time to talk much at all, save for a literal minute in the mornings when she dropped by for her coffee before having to bail almost immediately and a handful of texts throughout the day.

I didn't know what was worse—not knowing who that guy was to her, or having my fears confirmed that he *was* someone to her. Even though there was nothing romantic going on between Everly and me, I knew throwing an outside relationship into the mix would put an end to what we had. Maybe not immediately, and maybe not intentionally, but eventually, it would. And I knew that because if *I* were her boyfriend, there was no fucking way I'd be okay with her having the kind of relationship we shared with another man. Not even a little.

But I sure as fuck wasn't going to mention that to Ford. He'd twist it around to be all about me—namely, that I was jealous because I wanted Everly for myself—instead of what he should be focusing on—namely, that this new guy was a complete spunktrumpet who wasn't good enough for her.

"Oh yeah?" he said. "Wonder what's been the holdup on her end. Maybe that guy's been keeping her busy, if you know what I mean." My idiot of a brother grinned and waggled his eyebrows, and I had to stop myself from punching him in the throat.

I pointed the top of my water bottle toward him and narrowed my eyes. "Keep that shit up, and you're cut off."

"Look, all I'm saying is—"

"It's only been a couple days, and we've both just been busy, all right? If it's not a ridiculously overbooked schedule on her end, it's our dictator of a sister orchestrating every goddamn second of my day on mine."

Ford hummed in acknowledgment and relaxed back in the chair. "Addison *has* been a little dictatory lately, hasn't she? She's been working me to the bone. My lists have lists, for fuck's sake."

"She doesn't trust me with a list," I said. "She just points and barks orders and expects me to follow."

"Sounds on-brand for her. What's on the docket this week?"

"These stupid welcome baskets for all the guests. Since when do we do welcome baskets? It's fucking ridiculous.

They've got a whole goddamn ocean to welcome them. My blueberry oatmeal bars aren't going to push the experience over the top."

"I don't know. Those bars are fucking delicious. You got any leftovers?"

I rolled my eyes but reached into the cupboard and grabbed one of the wrapped bars I'd stashed for him before tossing it his way.

"Nice." He grinned. "Be glad that's all she's had you working on. For the past three days, she's had me sanding decks. By hand." He shook his head, face drawn. "She's becoming too powerful. We should probably do something about that."

We stared at each other, both taking a sip of our respective drinks, then shrugged at the same time.

"Not worth the fight," I said.

"Nope. So I guess it's a lifetime of servitude to our baby sister."

"Beats a lifetime of payback from her."

"That's the truth. So…" he said, drawing out the word. "You think maybe Everly's purposely keeping this guy from you?"

"How'd we go from talking about Addison to talking about that guy again?" I thought we were done discussing the shithead.

He shrugged. "Just wondering."

"She brought him to the diner, so your theory's flawed."

"She brought him, yes, but she never mentioned him. Didn't set anything up with you to meet him or hang out. And she's weirdly been busy this week..."

I didn't want to talk about this. Mostly because I didn't want to face the war going on inside me over the fact that I couldn't decide if I hated or loved that she hadn't told me anything about him. While I had no desire to find out any more about that guy, it was odd not knowing absolutely everything that was going on in Everly's life. She told me everything big or small—if Chuckanut kept her up an hour later than usual or when she got her IUD replaced or if she stubbed her toe—hell, I knew her damn cycle—but she couldn't tell me she was dating someone? That shit hurt, whether or not I'd admit it aloud.

"But it's probably better that way," he said.

I snapped my head in his direction. "What? Why?"

He lifted a shoulder. "So you don't go all jealous caveman on him and ruin her new relationship."

Those last two words in reference to Everly made something dark twist in my gut. I hated the thought of her with someone... No, not with *someone*. With *that guy*. If it'd been anyone else, I would've been okay with it if it made her happy because she, more than anyone, deserved that. But that she'd picked such a jackass who didn't pay her an ounce of attention didn't sit well with me. She deserved a hell of a lot better than what he was giving her.

"I don't know why no one else can see that he's not the

right one for her," I snapped. "He's a dick. You think she belongs with a dick?"

Ford stared at me, one brow raised, and for once, I had no idea what he was thinking. "Well...you've been called a dick a time or two."

"What the hell does that have to do with—"

But before I could finish my question, the radio crackled to life, the disembodied voice on the other end calling for all available units to an address I knew by heart, and my whole fucking world stopped.

THE DRIVE to Everly's house was the longest six minutes of my life, especially because Ford had taken my keys and shoved me in the passenger's seat so I couldn't control the speed or the route. I'd never felt fear like I had when he'd confirmed that I'd heard what I thought I had—a possible structure fire with unknown occupancy at Everly's home. Well, maybe once... Almost a decade ago, during the storm when Mom went missing and then the subsequent hours until the boat was found. Empty.

I couldn't handle another outcome like that. Not now. Not with Everly.

I wasn't a glass half-full kind of guy. I was a *tell it like it is, don't sugarcoat it, and keep your rose-colored glasses 'cause I don't need them* kind of guy. And right now, I hated that that was who I was. Because though I wanted to believe everything was fine, that she was okay, an image of her house, engulfed in flames, played on a loop in my mind, and nothing I could do put an end to it.

"Can't you drive any fucking faster?" I barked, clenching my hands into fists as my body vibrated with the urge to do *something*.

"Going as fast as I can, man." How could his voice be so fucking calm when it felt like my entire world was spinning out of control?

When he finally screeched to a halt half a block away from Everly's, thanks to the cluster of emergency vehicles gathered in front, I barely waited for the truck to come to a stop before I was out the door.

While my imagination had run wild on the way over there, the actual sight of flames licking up the side of her perfect little house would haunt me forever. The vise grip on my heart tightened, squeezing to the point of pain. I couldn't fucking breathe, fear over where she was, whether she was hurt or safe, overwhelming me.

It was chaos everywhere I turned—too many people and none of them *her*. I needed to find Everly. To make sure she was okay. That she wasn't still inside. *Jesusfuck*, what if she was still—

"Over there." Ford gripped my shoulders and turned me away from Everly's burning home and toward the woman herself. She sat in the back of an ambulance, blanket wrapped around her and Chuckanut, who sat calmly in her lap, like their home wasn't burning behind them. She wore an oversized T-shirt—one of mine I must've accidentally left at one time or another—and little else, her bare legs peeking out from beneath the blanket, her face smeared with soot.

I inhaled sharply, the clamp around my heart loosening, and stumbled, feeling like I could finally breathe for the first time since the call had come across the radio. The urge to go to her, to hold her and reassure myself she was here and safe and in one piece, overwhelmed me, and for once, I didn't question or try to shove it away as I ran to her.

As if she could sense me, she lifted her head, her eyes locking on mine, and everything in me settled. Maybe for her, too, because as soon as she saw me, her shoulders sagged and her lip quivered, the blank mask she wore cracking as her eyes filled with tears.

"B-Beck," she choked out, and someone might as well have shoved a knife straight through my heart. It would've hurt less.

"Sunshine..." I could barely get out the single word, my voice scraped raw. I cupped her face, brushed her disheveled hair back, held her shoulders, and checked her over from head to toe, though I had no idea what I was looking for. I turned to the EMT—Ben Adams, who was barely out of diapers—hovering on her left. "Who's taking care of her?" I tried to ask the question calmly, but from the look on Ben's face, it hadn't come out that way.

With wide eyes, he raised his hand like he was still in

grade school. "Um, me. I am."

"No, you're not," I barked. "You're just standing there while her fucking teeth are chattering."

"I—I already—"

"If she's not in perfect condition, I'm holding you personally responsible, do you understand?"

"But I—I can't—"

"Hey, Ben," Ford said as he clapped the incompetent EMT on the shoulder, cool, calm, and collected, as if I hadn't been minutes away from losing one of the most important people in my life. "What my brother means to say is—"

Nope, I meant to say exactly what I did, but I didn't care how Ford smoothed that over. All I cared about was Everly. I refocused my attention on her as she gazed up at me, twin tear tracks streaking through the soot on her face.

"It's okay. You're okay," I said quietly just to her. I didn't know if I was trying to reassure her or myself, but I kept repeating the words, nonetheless, catching her tears with my thumbs as she shivered, her teeth chattering. "Jesus, don't you have another fucking blanket?" I snapped at Ben. "She doesn't even have any goddamn pants on."

"I'm wearing sh-shorts," she said, a shudder racking her body as she pulled the blanket tighter around her.

"It's the adrenaline crash, man," Ford said, clapping me on the shoulder. "She should head to the hospital to get checked out, but she'll be all right."

"I'm f-f-fine," Everly said, barely able to get out the

word.

Like hell she was.

"You're not fucking fine." And these idiots were taking too goddamn long to grab her another blanket. Instead of waiting, I scooped her up in my arms—Chuck and all— and settled her sideways in my lap as I sat where she'd just been. Shaking like a leaf, she curled against me, laying her head on my chest as I draped the blanket over her and held her and Chuck as tightly as I dared. "You can either go to the hospital in the back of the ambulance or in my truck, but you're going one way or another."

"St-still b-barking orders, even after a f-f-fire. At least you're c-consistent."

Ben cleared his throat. "I highly suggest she go via—"

"Nobody asked you," I snapped. "She's going to get there however she wants."

Ben held up his hands with a shake of his head. "Whatever you say. Just let me know if I'm transporting her."

I lowered my head and murmured against her ear, "What's it going to be, sunshine?"

She tightened her fingers in my shirt, and I took that as my cue to hold her tighter. "W-with you."

And then she ducked her head, resting her cheek on my chest as I buried my nose in her hair and breathed her in. She smelled sharply of smoke and nothing like the subtle floral scent she usually did, but I inhaled deeply anyway. That scent reminded me she was okay. She was still here with me, and I had no intention of letting her go.

CHAPTER SEVEN

EVERLY

AFTER MY BRIEF checkup at the hospital, Beck drove us toward the resort. He kept stealing glances at me, as if he were checking to make sure I was still there, right where he left me. He hadn't gone so far as three feet away from me since he'd shown up at the fire. Either I was in his lap or next to him or he was pacing a couple feet away and glaring as the doctor or nurses looked me over. Some people might have felt smothered by that, but not me. Not with him.

If it were my brother or my parents, I would've felt the need to be strong. To prove I had it all together and I didn't need any help. That I was totally and completely fine, despite all that'd happened tonight.

With Beck, I could just be me.

More than that, I didn't even have to voice what I needed—he always just seemed to know.

I wasn't sure if it'd been his scary eyes, his barked commands, or something else entirely, but I'd received excellent care—and a pair of scrubs to change into—at the hospital and had been given the all clear to go home.

Except I didn't have a home to go back to anymore.

Ford, who'd offered to take Chuckanut with him for the night since we had no idea how long I'd be at the hospital, had called while I'd been getting checked out and let us know what was going on. The fire was out, and while the firefighters had been able to stop the flames from engulfing the clinic, my house was unlivable, if still standing, and there was at least smoke damage, if not more, to the rest of the dwelling.

I'd never been so happy to have fallen asleep on the couch downstairs instead of up in my bedroom as I was tonight. I'd been able to escape out of the house with Chuckanut under my arm, only obtaining a couple scrapes on my hands and some minor smoke inhalation that was more of a nuisance than anything. And thankfully, I hadn't had any late-night appointments or overnight guests at the clinic.

I stared out the window while Beck drove, his hand resting in my lap as I held it tightly between mine. Even though it was too dark outside to see anything, I imagined the ocean spread out in front of us and the waves crashing against the shore. That was one thing I didn't love about my home—it wasn't on the beach. The rhythmic sound of the ocean always lulled me into serenity, so at least I'd have that while I stayed at the resort and figured out what the hell to do next.

Beck pulled to a stop and turned off the truck with his left hand, leaving his right encased in mine. I glanced up, expecting to see the main inn, except we were behind the diner at the back entrance to his apartment.

"Why are we here?" I asked, my voice scratchy and raw. "I still need to get checked in."

"The fuck you do," he said, the words coming out as a sharp demand. He'd been in his default barking mode tonight, but I wasn't surprised. That was his go-to when he didn't feel completely in control. And there was no way he'd feel in control of this. I'd never seen him look so disheveled when he'd shown up at the fire, his face drained of color as he'd frantically searched the area for me.

Because I knew he was dealing with this in his own way, I just raised a brow in response.

He closed his eyes, pinching the bridge of his nose as he inhaled deeply before slowly releasing it. Then, in a calmer tone than he'd used before, he said, "You're staying with me."

"Beck, I don't—"

"You're staying with me," he said again, his voice firm but not quite the sharp command it had been.

I'd been to Beck's place more times than I could count —his recliners were perfect for movie nights—same as he'd been to mine, but this felt different. And there was the small issue that his apartment had a single bedroom and no couch, just two comfortable as all get-out leather chairs. But that was a problem for Future Everly to face. Present Everly was too exhausted to worry about it.

"Okay."

He must've been preparing for a fight because his whole body relaxed at the single word. "Okay?"

"Yeah, okay."

"Right, okay, great." He jumped out of the truck and was around to my side before I could even fumble with the handle to get the door opened. "C'mon." And then he reached over, unbuckled my seat belt, and lifted me straight into his arms, kicking the door shut behind us as he carried me up the steps to his apartment.

"Are you serious right now?"

"What?" Brows pinched, he glanced down at me, the sharp angles of his face so much more pronounced in the shadows.

"I can walk."

"You don't have any shoes, remember?"

No, actually, I hadn't remembered, and my throat tightened as I tried to swallow around the lump lodged there. The fire had been so hot already when I'd woken up, too close to do anything but grab Chuckanut and run. I hadn't been able to save anything from my house—not pictures or the quilt my mom had made me or Aunt Shirley's string of pearls—except my dog and my phone that'd been right next to me. Which meant I didn't have any shoes at all anymore. I didn't have *anything* at all anymore.

Beck made a gruff sound in the back of his throat as he stared down at me. "I'll take care of it."

I knew he would—that was Beck for you—but I couldn't find my voice to tell him it was about so much more than the shoes. My whole life had just gone up in flames—literally—and where did that leave me? Instead of telling him any of that, I just swallowed down my tears and nodded as he guided us into his space. He set me down on the kitchen counter, then braced his palms on either side of my hips. His hands were curled into fists, his face tight, and tension radiated from the stiff line of his shoulders.

And because he wouldn't initiate anything but I could tell this was something he needed just as much as I did, I wrapped myself around him and held him to me. He was frozen for a few seconds, then his body relaxed as he brought his arms around me, enveloping me in warmth and comfort, and I breathed in his scent that I'd come to think of as home.

It could've been minutes or seconds later when he pulled away to grab me a water out of the fridge. "Drink this."

I mock saluted him but took the proffered bottle anyway because my throat was killing me. "Thanks."

"It's late, but do you need to call the douchebag and let him know I've got this under control?"

I froze with the water bottle halfway to my mouth and stared at him, my brows raised. "The who?"

"The *douchebag*," he enunciated. "Seymour."

"I have no idea who you're talking about."

"The guy. Sean. Seth. Samuel. Whatever—that guy from the diner." His jaw ticked. "The one who was at your house."

A raspy laugh burst free. "*Sebastian*?" I shook my head, grateful for this moment of levity after such a harrowing night and clinging to it. I could use a little redirection to focus on right now. "Honestly, what's up with you two? I thought you'd get along a lot better than you did."

He stared at me like I'd grown two heads. "Why the fuck would you think that?"

"Well, I don't know." I shrugged. "I've been talking about you both to each other for two years, and it's been fine. And then, all of a sudden—"

"Whoa, whoa, wait. What the hell do you mean, you've been talking to me about him? I have no idea who that guy is."

"Um, yes, you do."

"Sunshine. I promise you I don't."

"And I promise you do. It's Ash."

Shaking his head, he furrowed his brow. "I thought you said it was Sebastian."

"Right," I said slowly. "Also known as Ash. My brother?"

He stared at me for a long moment, his mouth hanging

open, and then the scowl was back in full force. "Then why the hell did he introduce himself as Sebastian?"

"Because that's his name."

He pressed his palms to his eyes and groaned. "Jesus, Everly, I feel like we're talking in circles. If his name is Sebastian, why the hell do you call him Ash?"

I shrugged. "Couldn't pronounce it when I was little, and Ash just stuck."

"But he's in your phone as Sebastian."

I raised a brow, wondering how he knew that but ultimately didn't care. I'd tossed him my phone more times than I could count, and he knew my passcode same as I knew his, so it wasn't like anything was a secret on there. "That's a long but entertaining story involving a mistaken and very blunt text meant for one of my girlfriends in college. He threatened me with banishment if I didn't change how he was listed because of the mix-up." I tipped my head to the side. "How'd you know what he's listed as in my phone?"

He grunted and looked anywhere but at me. "I saw it when you were trying to text Ford."

"So you've spent the past few days thinking he was...what?"

"A really shitty boyfriend." He scowled, like the words themselves had personally offended him.

I laughed again, this time spiraling into a coughing fit. The doctor had said this was to be expected and would go away soon, along with the soreness in my throat. I may have coughing bouts from time to time, but I only needed to come back in if anything worsened.

Apparently Beck hadn't heard that part of the doctor's speech because he shoved my water bottle at me, face drawn in a scowl, and barked, "Drink."

I rolled my eyes but took a small sip, raising my brows at him until he grunted his approval. Once I could speak again, I said, "Definitely not a boyfriend. Just my pain-in-the-ass little brother who made an impromptu trip to escape his recent breakup. So, you officially hate the only member of my family you've met."

"I don't hate him," he mumbled, not meeting my eyes.

"Well, the reception was a little cold, even for you." I sighed, shoulders slumping at the thought of having to tell them about tonight. They already weren't thrilled with my being here—as Ash had very bluntly pointed out before he'd left—but I'd felt coming here and taking over the clinic was what I'd needed to do for Aunt Shirley. Regardless, it was not going to be a fun conversation. "I need to call him and my parents."

Luckily, I still had my phone so I could do so, but that was all I had to my name. My single possession was a four-year-old smartphone with a cracked screen. I wasn't even sure my car had avoided damage with how fast the fire had spread. And just the thought of telling my brother and parents all of that exhausted me.

I loved my family—how could I not? They were great, but sometimes, it felt more like I was performing a part in a play when I was around them—my parents, especially—than I was actually living my life. I'd crafted so much of myself in an effort to make them proud of me, I often wondered if the things I liked now were things I *actually* enjoyed or if I'd conditioned myself to.

"But I don't want to call them tonight," I admitted barely above a whisper.

"Then you don't have to," Beck said with so little fanfare but with utter finality, I had to admire him. He didn't soften his edges or bend to the will of anyone. People got him completely as he was, or they didn't get him at all.

I loved his harshness, his gruff exterior, the tough shell he worked hard to maintain. Because it made the glimpses of that soft, gooey center all the more rewarding.

"C'mon." He gripped my hips and tugged me off the counter, then guided me to his bathroom. "You'll feel better after a shower. Towels are in the closet. We can wash those scrubs tomorrow. I'll, uh... I'll grab you something to wear tonight."

I was so tired, but a shower sounded heavenly, especially since I was still filthy and smelled like...well, like I'd just escaped a house fire. Would it be weird to ask him to stay in here with me? Probably, since the shower had a see-through glass enclosure that would leave absolutely no mystery between besties. So I nodded, and he stepped out of the room, his eyes briefly locking with mine in the mirror just before the door latched behind him.

Exhaling a heavy sigh, I braced my hands on the sink and hung my head. There was so much to do, so many calls to make, so many things to replace, I didn't even know where to start.

But I could get to all that tomorrow. Right now, all I needed was a shower and a heaping dose of Beck's personal brand of comfort.

CHAPTER EIGHT

EVERLY

TWENTY MINUTES and five hair washes later, I was fresh and clean and...still smelling faintly of smoke. I had no idea how long I'd be giving off that campfire aroma or how many showers I'd have to take before the scent would completely disappear, but I hoped it wouldn't linger for too long. I didn't want the constant reminder of what'd happened tonight clinging to me while I tried to figure out what I was going to do.

Magically, a stack of Beck's clothes had been waiting for me just outside the bathroom door when I'd opened it, wrapped up in one of his surprisingly plush towels. I tucked myself back inside and slipped into the garments, letting his familiar scent wash over me and comfort me in a way I hadn't anticipated needing. Tears pricked the backs of my eyes, but I didn't let them fall as I pulled on one of his T-shirts and stepped into the pair of far-too-long sweatpants sans panties—I was going to have to go commando until I could replace my undergarments. Wearing his clothes felt like a constant hug, and I'd take all the hugs I could get right now.

I didn't think the full impact of what had happened had even registered completely, but these waves of emotions still washed over me at random times, the despair over all I'd lost nearly overwhelming. But I'd figure out a way to get through it. I always did.

Once I was dressed, I padded out into the main area. Beck's apartment was nice. Tidy without being rigid— there was a stack of mail on the counter, the book we'd been reading this week on a side table, and a couple pairs of shoes haphazardly tossed by the door—and warm without being stuffy. But it was small, just a bedroom, bathroom, and one main room that held a galley-style kitchen and the living area, which housed only two leather recliners, a small table between them both, and a TV large enough to fit right at home in a sports bar. Luckily, the loungers were super comfortable, so Beck could sleep in his room, and I could stay out here by myself.

Except...I didn't want to.

My entire life, I'd prided myself on my independence. I was the kid who'd been babysitting by the age of eight and helping prepare dinners by the time I was ten. I was the self-starter who entertained herself and took care of what was needed without any reminders. I'd always just... handled things. But right now, after experiencing the scariest night of my life? I didn't want to handle things by myself. I didn't want to be alone.

At the creak of the floor, Beck turned his chair around to face me, his gaze roving over me from head to toe in an appraisal that felt weighted. His eyes were a little more scrutinizing, his gaze a little more intense. A shiver racked my body—no doubt a lingering effect from my earlier adrenaline crash—and I wrapped my arms around myself so he didn't get an unwanted eyeful of my nipples.

He lifted his chin toward the small end table between the chairs. "Made you a grilled cheese. You need to eat."

I didn't want to mention that it was after midnight or that I wasn't hungry. In the years we'd been friends, I'd come to realize how he showed he cared was through cooking, so I was going to eat it—as much of it as I could, anyway. Especially when he'd made my number one comfort food—which he always fancied up with Parmesan-crusted homemade bread—and especially because I knew he must be crawling out of his skin right now, not knowing how to help.

Five minutes ago, I might not have known how he could help, either. But right then, it was clear as day. I needed my person, and that just happened to be the grump who'd reluctantly let me into his life, little by little, because I hadn't allowed it any other way.

He glanced over at my chair—yes, mine. The one I sat in every Wednesday as we worked our way through old classic shows and every Sunday for book club and nearly every Friday for movie night. My favorite blanket was piled in the seat, looking soft and comforting. But not as comforting as the gruff man with a permanent scowl on his face. Gone was the baseball hat he nearly always wore, and he'd changed into a T-shirt and sweats—both of which looked just as cozy as my blanket.

So instead of sitting in my usual spot, I walked straight to him, ignoring the nest he'd built for me, and dropped into his lap, tucking my legs up to my chest and resting my head on his shoulder. This was no longer new for us. It'd taken some time, but we were officially over that awkward stage I'd thrown us into in the first place. The first time I'd hugged him, he'd stood there, completely frozen and arms hanging limply at his sides, until I'd laughed and physically wrapped them around me and told him to squeeze. Every time after had gotten a bit easier, and now it was a given that he was getting a hug hello and a hug goodbye and that we'd probably also have some sort of cuddle in the middle.

But now, he froze beneath me, his entire body going rigid, hands gripping the chair arms, and I wondered if I'd finally pushed too far. I might have needed that physical comfort, but it'd been a long night for him, too, and maybe he just wanted to be left alone. And, well, I was just going to have to deal with it.

"Sorry, I'll—" I shifted to get off his lap when he set his hands on me, holding me in place.

"Don't," he said, his voice gruff and low. Goose bumps

erupted on my skin when I settled back into him, his body heat a stark contrast to my other side.

When I didn't make a move to get up, he plucked the blanket from the other chair and draped it over me, nestling me in against him. Then he grabbed the plate of grilled cheese and put it right under my nose. "Eat."

"Have we entered the single-syllable part of the night?"

"What? No."

I giggled as I took a small bite of the sandwich. "That might've been two words, but still only a single syllable each."

"Don't make me feed you."

I tipped my head back and grinned up at him, which earned me an eye roll in response. As Beck turned on the TV and cued up the search bar to find us something to watch, I ate my sandwich, nixing every suggestion he gave —all seven of them.

"I don't know why you do this to yourself," I said. "I always want to watch the same thing after a rough day. And I'd say this was pretty rough."

His chest lifted with a deep inhale, and I pressed my lips together to hide my smile. "You're really going to make me watch *Gossip Girl* at one o'clock in the morning?"

"You can pretend you don't like it all you want, but don't think I haven't noticed how you shush me if I try to talk during it."

"I shush you when you try to talk during anything. Which is always, by the way."

"But if I didn't talk, how would I irritate you?"

"I'm sure you'd find a way."

I grinned down at my plate and heard the familiar opening chords to *Gossip Girl*. I didn't know what I'd done to deserve this kind of friendship, but I would forever be grateful. I could spend the rest of my life thanking Beck for being there for me while I stumbled through these past two years on my own, away from all my family and friends, and it still wouldn't be enough.

I tipped my head back to tell him as much at the same time he turned toward me, but instead of his lips landing on my forehead like he'd no doubt intended, they pressed softly against mine. We both stilled, our mouths connected, eyes wide on each other. His lips were soft, his breath warm, and it all felt so good and safe and comforting that my lids fluttered closed and I melted into him, pressing my lips more firmly against his. I exhaled a sigh and swiped my tongue out to lick a soft path against his lower lip, and that simple, subtle movement was like a gunshot in the room.

With a groan, he cupped my face and held me tight as he kissed me back. His mouth was hot and hungry on mine, as if he couldn't get enough of my taste, and all I could do was grip the front of his T-shirt and hold on for the ride. He tilted my head how he wanted, swept his tongue into my mouth, and kissed me like I'd never been kissed before. With desperation and want and so much desire it left me breathless.

I couldn't believe this was Beck—*my Beck*—kissing the absolute life out of me, and I was loving every second of it. My *God*, how had I not known my best friend was a kissing prodigy?

He pulled away only long enough to scrape his teeth against my lower lip, his tongue laving the sting before he dove right back in all over again, and I was a puddle of pure need in his lap. Without breaking the kiss, I discarded my plate on the table and shifted around so I could straddle him, the blanket falling on the floor as I settled myself over the very thick, very hard bulge in his sweatpants. Our groans mixed together as I rocked against him, desperate to be closer, for the clothes between us to disappear, to *really* feel him. To find out what else I didn't know about this man.

I wasn't sure how long we sat there making out like teenagers, only that I had no intention of stopping. Not when I was finally getting a taste of what every romance I'd ever read had talked about but which I'd never experienced in my life. Eventually, though, Beck pulled away, still cupping my face, and rested his forehead against mine. His eyes were closed as we both tried to catch our breath.

But I didn't want to catch my breath. I wanted to lose it all over again.

"Why'd you stop?" I whispered, my hands somehow resting on his stomach beneath his shirt—when had that happened?—his skin an inferno beneath my palms.

"We can't do this now," he said, his voice like gravel. "Not tonight. Not after—"

He swallowed, his eyes haunted, and I nodded, even though I wasn't very happy about it. The state of my pussy *definitely* wasn't happy about it. But he had a point. Tonight had been a *lot*. If—*when*—Beck and I did this again, I didn't want any lingering doubts or hesitations. Nothing he could angst over as he was known to do.

"Okay." I twisted back around and settled sideways in his lap, draping my legs over his, still very aware of how hard he was beneath me and trying to ignore the dampness in my borrowed pants. "Not tonight."

He may have put the brakes on for right now, but now that I knew how he kissed, knew he liked it when I tugged on his lower lip and threaded my fingers through his hair and rocked against him hard enough for us both to gasp, I was definitely exploring that.

He grabbed the blanket from the floor, pressed a kiss to my temple, and restarted *Gossip Girl.* Then he wrapped his arms around me and held me as the show played in the background and I tried to come to terms with the fact that a single kiss had just shaken up everything I'd thought I'd known—both about the supposed intimacy I'd had in my life *and* about my best friend. And though this day had been the worst day of my life without a doubt, maybe something good could come from it after all.

I fell asleep with Beck's arms around me, his warmth against my side and his heartbeat beneath my ear.

CHAPTER NINE

BECK

AFTER TOO FEW HOURS, I woke to find Everly still asleep in my lap, her cheek resting on my chest. She was curled up against me, so peaceful and trusting, and knowing that only thrust the knife deeper into my gut. Because all I could think about was her throaty little moans from last night and how pretty she'd look taking my cock.

Christ. What the fuck had I done?

I didn't make friends easily. Hell, I didn't make friends at all. I was a private guy who didn't let anyone inside the inner circle that currently held only Ford—not even the rest of my siblings had made it through that door. But Everly hadn't let that stop her. She'd barreled her way into my life and hadn't let up since, a one-woman bulldozer. She was the first person outside of family not to be put off by my demeanor. The best thing that had happened to me in years.

And I'd gone and fucked it up last night. All because she made my dick hard—which wasn't news to me. The proof of that was wedged against my stomach, thick and throbbing as the weight of her pressed into it.

She deserved better than this. She deserved someone who wouldn't take advantage of her when she was at her lowest. Who wouldn't devour her on a goddamn chair two hours after her house had caught on fire. *Jesus.* I needed to get my shit together and be that man for her—the best friend she'd come to count on—and not just some guy with a hard-on who wanted to fuck her. I was her only support in Starlight Cove, and I'd just jeopardized that for a quick make-out session.

I needed some space to clear my head, but I wasn't going to leave her. I couldn't—not just for her peace of mind, but for mine. Which left me only one option—a shower. And from the state of my dick, I could certainly use one.

Thankfully, Everly slept like the dead, so when I stood with her in my arms, she didn't stir. And she didn't so much as twitch when I set her back on the chair and draped the blanket over her before silently making my way to the bathroom.

Once inside, I stripped and climbed into the shower, not bothering to wait for the water to heat up. Maybe the jolt in temperature would knock some sense into me.

What the hell had I been thinking? She'd just lost every-thing—*everything*—she had, and I'd shoved my tongue down her throat. Had settled my hands on her hips and guided her hot little pussy over me until I was nearly ready to explode in my pants like a goddamn teenager.

With a growl of frustration, I grabbed the soap and started scrubbing, as if that would absolve me of the memories from last night. But the scent did nothing to dissuade my throbbing cock, recalling the smell of it on Everly. Great. So now I was going to get hard every time I washed myself, like Pavlov's fucking dog.

When Everly had dropped into my lap last night, smelling like me, wearing my clothes, and looking like a fucking wet dream, all bright eyes and pouty lips, it'd taken all I had to stay still. To not move a fucking inch. I hadn't known what to do or how to respond—what was appropriate in that situation, 'cause I sure as fuck didn't know. But then her uncertainty had taken the uncertainty out of it for me, because I'd be whatever she needed me to be—always had, always would. And at that point, she'd needed my comfort.

So I'd wrapped my arms around her and prayed she hadn't noticed my cock growing harder with every second that passed. That had lasted all of three minutes before catastrophe struck.

One press of her lips against mine, and I was a changed man.

But still, I held back, refusing to cross that line after

what she'd been through. She'd been scared and anxious and had probably still been in shock.

Never mind the timid little way her tongue had peeked out, swiping against my lip. Or how she'd squirmed in my lap, like she'd spread her legs and sit right on my cock if I guided her to.

I muttered a curse, forcing myself back to the present. Bracing my hands on the tile wall, I clenched my eyes shut as if that would be enough to will away the memory of her taste. As if I could force my cock to deflate simply by shoving those thoughts aside. But there was no erasing those memories, because no matter what I did, the image of her haunted me—cheeks flushed, eyes bright, lips swollen from my kiss. From my teeth and my tongue.

I couldn't deny anymore that I wanted to see my marks all over her. Wanted to bite and suck down the long column of her neck. Wanted to lick across her collarbones, suck those perfect tits into my mouth, and devour her pussy.

But it was wrong. I shouldn't be thinking about my best friend that way. Shouldn't be fantasizing about her in the shower with me, on her knees as she took me deep into her mouth, all the way to her throat, her eyes wide and innocent while she choked on my cock.

I shouldn't be, but I was.

With a growl, I wrapped my hand around my shaft and gripped tightly. I swallowed a groan as I stroked up the length, imagining her hands, her mouth, her pussy on me. Imagining the two of us recreating Chapter Twenty-Two, her spread out on my bed, blindfolded and bound and begging for my cock. Then it switched to last week's book—Chapter Seventeen—watching as Everly got herself off with a toy while I directed how fast and how hard and how much. Then it was Chapter Twelve of the first book we'd read together, bending her over a balcony above a busy street and fucking her where anyone could see.

My balls started to tingle, my impending orgasm breathing down my neck. I closed my eyes and groaned, hoping she didn't hear me over the sound of the spray. Hoping she was still asleep and would never know anything about this. I could just pretend it never happened. Pretend I hadn't tasted ambrosia on her tongue last night. Pretend it hadn't felt like everything had slid into place when she'd straddled my lap and rocked against me, my name a breathy sigh on her lips. Pretend she hadn't completely fucking changed me.

I had to. Because if I didn't, there was only destruction ahead of us. Only heartbreak and a messy end to what we had. And I wasn't ready to give her up. Not yet. Not ever.

As my orgasm pressed down on me, I tightened my grip around my cock, swiping my thumb across the head as I quickened my strokes and replayed that sweet little moan she'd breathed straight into my mouth. I imagined it was the heat of her pussy surrounding me instead of the poor substitute of my hand, and that was all it took. I groaned her name as I came, spilling over my fingers to thoughts of her coming around me.

A sharp gasp sounded in the room, and I snapped my eyes open, whipping my head toward the door even as shudders still racked my body. And there she stood, lip caught between her teeth and eyes wide as she drank me in from head to toe. The glass shower doors hid absolutely nothing from her, least of all my hand wrapped around my cock as I coaxed out the last ripple of my orgasm.

"Sunshine," I choked out, bracing myself on the wall.

"Oh my God. Am I still dreaming?" she asked, her voice raspy.

"I—"

"'Cause I just had a dream about you." She took another step closer, her eyes glued on my cock, and the greedy bastard was already kicking back to life at her attention. "But you didn't look like that."

I swallowed, sure I was going to regret asking this, but I couldn't help myself. "How did I look?"

"Well, for starters"—she licked her lips—"you definitely weren't that big."

"Jesus, Everly," I groaned. "You can't say shit like that to me."

"Why not?"

"Because we're friends. You're not supposed to— We're not—"

"We did last night."

"We shouldn't have."

Her eyes flashed up to mine, and she squared her shoulders, determination written in her gaze. "You didn't like it?"

"Christ." I squeezed my eyes shut, curling my hand into a fist as I braced it against the tile. "Of course I fucking liked it. You just watched me come all over my hand to memories of it."

She breathed out a breathy little, "Oh," as she licked her lips, her gaze darting between my eyes and where my cock jutted toward her. "That was to thoughts of me?"

The correct answer was no. It was what I should've said, and then I should've turned my back on her and shut down this thing we'd started before it could go too far. Before either of us got hurt. My mind warred with itself, half of it wanting nothing more than to tell her to get out so we could salvage this friendship that meant everything to me, while the other half was desperate to invite her in to join me.

But it wouldn't have mattered what I said, because Everly made the decision for us both. She whipped the shirt over her head and allowed her borrowed pants to drop from her waist, exposing her completely to me, every inch of her on display.

"Oh fuck," I breathed, too stunned to say anything else.

She was gorgeous, her hair a riot of flames around her face, freckles scattered across her body—ones I'd known and seen and touched before, and ones that were all new that I wanted to map with my fingers and my tongue. Her nipples were the same shade as her lips, and *Jesusfuck*, I'd never be able to look at her smiling mouth again without seeing her perfect tits and imagining them in my mouth.

"You said, 'not tonight.'" She took a step toward me. "Well...it's not tonight..."

CHAPTER TEN

EVERLY

I THOUGHT I WAS DREAMING.

Though that wasn't too far of a stretch since I *had* been dreaming about Beck. But in it, we'd picked up right where we'd left off last night when I'd been settled in his lap. Only this time, we didn't have those pesky things called clothes between us. I'd been able to see all of him, and Dream Beck was gorgeous, all sinewy lines and harsh angles and a cock that was big without being intimidating.

But Dream Beck had *nothing* on the real thing. My subconscious hadn't properly filled in the sharp cut of his biceps, the thick ropes of muscle in his thighs, the definition of his abs, or the dusting of hair on his chest and the trail that led straight down to his... Yeah, that was *definitely* intimidating. More so because it was still hard and proud, jutting from his body even after he'd just come.

I'd always known Beck was gorgeous, with his short

beard covering a chiseled jaw, his perpetually shaggy thick, dark hair, and those *lips*... Early on, I'd put him in the *do not touch* box because of my circumstances, and that was where he'd stayed. But now? Seeing him like this? I'd never wanted to touch someone more in my life, and this was my *best friend*. What kind of alternate universe had I stepped into? If I took a second to think about what I was doing in here, I'd probably talk myself out of this. I didn't do rash, and I didn't do casual, and I certainly didn't see my friends naked.

But everything had changed last night—not just following the fire, but following the kiss that had shaken my very foundation.

Every other relationship I'd ever had had been easy. Predictable. *Boring.* But the twenty minutes I'd spent making out with Beck last night had been...enlightening. He'd evoked more of a reaction from me in those handful of minutes than my last boyfriend had over the course of *years*. And if I didn't explore whatever this was between us, I'd regret it for the rest of my life.

I knew Beck well enough to realize he'd never take that step without my offering, though. Not after what I'd been through last night. In fact, he was probably beating himself up for even allowing us to kiss after the day I'd had. But last night had sparked something inside me— something I wanted to explore for myself. And for once, I wanted to be selfish and see where it took me with no ulterior motive but my own pleasure.

As I stepped out of his clothes and stood before him completely naked, raw desire emanated from his eyes, and the part of me that'd been nervous to put myself out there, only to be rejected, breathed a sigh of relief. He was ravenous for me, and he didn't try to hide an ounce of it as he let his gaze trail over my body, eyes zeroing in on all the places that ached for his touch.

"Sunshine," he croaked, the single word a strangled plea, and I couldn't stop myself from going to him even if I'd wanted to.

I slid open the glass door and entered the shower stall, the water warming my back while Beck's gaze heated my front. He stepped back, allowing me room as he licked his lips and looked his fill of me, eyes blazing.

"You're so fucking gorgeous. How am I supposed to say no?" His voice was rough and ragged, so low and deep it slid over me like melted chocolate and seeped into my bones. He reached out and brushed his thumb across my lower lip, parting them for him. The urge to swipe my tongue against it and suck it into my mouth was automatic, so I did both, my body flushing at his answering groan. "Tell me how I'm supposed to turn you away when you come in here looking like a fucking dream and then suck the tip of my thumb like you wish it were my cock."

A shiver ran through me at his words, so blunt and raw —so unlike anything I'd ever heard in real life—and my pussy tingled at the thought of taking him in my mouth. Of sucking him deep and pleasuring him while he stared down at me like I was the most beautiful thing in the world.

"I don't want you to," I said, being as honest with him as I always was.

I stepped closer, dragging my fingers through the smattering of dark hair on his chest and down the corrugated hills and valleys of his abs. I'd touched him plenty over the course of our friendship. Innocent touches here and there, but never like this. Never so much bare skin, completely exposed to my fingers... I wanted to touch him *everywhere.* To explore and acquaint myself with all the parts of him I didn't know, that I'd never had the privilege of seeing before, every inch that was new to me. And there were a whole lot of new inches... Jesus, *that* was going to take some getting used to. His cock was long and so thick, I truly didn't know if he'd fit. I'd always thought it was cliché when a heroine wondered that in a book, but it was all fun and games until you were suddenly the one staring down the barrel of a Pringles can demanding entrance to your lady garden.

His cock twitched at my attention, and he groaned, spinning us around so I was out of the spray and pushing my back against the cold tile. He gripped my hips, his fingers digging into my flesh, as if he were trying to hold himself back. Then he dropped his face into my neck and inhaled deeply before dragging his lips over my skin, his teeth scraping along the juncture that had my nipples tightening into stiff peaks. His cock pressed against my hip, so thick and hard and flushed, and I had to push my hands against the wall to stop from reaching for him.

"I've tried, sunshine. I've tried so fucking hard to ignore this."

"Ignore what?" I asked, breathless as I tipped my head to the side and allowed him more access. Allowed him all the space he needed to torment me with his mouth, soft whispers of his lips followed by the sharp bite of his teeth, and then the slick heat of his tongue. I moaned, already wet for him, and we hadn't even really started.

"How fucking much I want you," he said, his words rough and low, as if the admission were pulled straight from his soul. He dipped his head then, sucking my nipple into his mouth hard enough to draw a gasp from me.

"*Beck.*" I threaded my fingers in his hair, holding him to me as he kissed and sucked my breasts. "I want that too."

I may not have realized it before, but there was no denying it now. I was drenched, my clit throbbing with a need that only increased with every flick of his tongue, every brush of his lips, every pass of his hands on my bare skin.

"Not yet." He cupped my breasts and lifted, pushing them together. Brushing his thumbs over my nipples, he locked his gaze with mine. Reading me. Studying my reactions. Making sure I was still with him in this strange new facet of our relationship.

And I was. I was *all* in.

When he pinched one of my nipples between his

thumb and forefinger and tugged, I gasped, arching toward him, and curled my fingers into his chest. "Yes yet. *Please.*"

He shook his head, eyes heavy-lidded, cock hard and thick between us. "You have no idea how long I've waited for this, so let me enjoy it."

"You've—" Before I could get out the rest of my question, he dropped to his knees, staring up at me with a glint in his eyes, and my stomach flipped like I'd just jumped out of an airplane.

"What're you doing?" I asked, nerves bubbling up as I stared down at him.

"It's been a while, but I thought that was pretty obvious."

"So you're going to, um..." I swallowed, attempting to generate some moisture in my mouth. "You want to..."

"Lick your pussy? Dying to."

"Oh," I breathed, the single syllable just an exhalation. I hadn't expected him to be so...blunt. "But this is— Well, I've never—"

My words stuck in my throat as he looked at me, brow raised. But how could I tell him I was a thirty-year-old woman who'd had multiple long-term partners but had never once received oral? And that even though the thought of it turned me on something fierce, there was still a big part of me that was nervous to do it here, in the light of day, where I was so spread out and vulnerable in front of him.

"You've never...?" he asked.

Oh my God, he was actually going to make me say it.

"I've never done..." My cheeks flamed as I gestured to his position, face inches from my pussy. "This."

His gaze heated. "Are you telling me no one's ever had their mouth on you?"

"No," I whispered, the sound barely audible over the shower spray.

"No one's sucked this pretty little clit?" He brushed his thumb over it, exposing me to him completely as he blew a gust of air against me.

I moaned and shuddered, shaking my head as I stared down at him with hooded eyes. "No."

"No one's ever tasted your sweet cunt?"

"No," I breathed, clit throbbing at the slightest attention he gave it, desperate for more.

"Is that because you don't want to?" he asked, though he could probably guess the answer to that, considering the number of books we read where the heroes went down on the heroines every chance they got, but I still answered him anyway.

"No, I do. I'm just...nervous."

He lifted one of my legs over his shoulder and looked up at me with a gleam in his eyes, and my nerves fluttered away at the pure hunger written on his face. Then he leaned forward, sucking on the crease of my leg—close but not nearly close enough—and I shuddered in response. "It's just me. And I'm going to show you exactly how this pussy deserves to be eaten. All you have to do is watch me worship every fucking inch of you."

With his eyes locked on mine, he licked a line straight up my center, flicking the tip of his tongue against my swollen clit, and my leg nearly gave out at the explosion of sensation that washed over me. I gasped, one hand flying to the wall for balance, while I gripped his hair with my other.

"That's right, sunshine," he said against me, dragging his bottom lip back and forth over my clit. "Move my mouth exactly where you want it. Use my tongue to get off. I want you to ride my face until you come all over it. I don't want to stop until I'm drowning in you."

"*Beck*. Oh my God, you can't talk like that."

He grinned against me, a devilish smirk I'd never seen on him, his eyes glinting. "Don't try to pretend you don't love every filthy word coming out of my mouth. I know exactly the kinds of books you read and exactly the dirty talk that gets you off." He swiped two fingers through my slit on either side of my clit, making me arch my hips toward him as I sought more. "But it's going to be *my* words tonight, sunshine. Now, rock your hips against my face just like that. Let me taste exactly how much you love my dirty mouth."

He slipped his fingers inside me, pumping them slowly at first, his movements growing faster with each moan that left my lips. He added a third, stretching me in the most delicious way as he lapped at my clit, flicking it with his tongue before sucking it into his mouth.

"That—" I choked out, tightening my fingers in his hair, desperate for him to keep doing *exactly* what he was doing, though I couldn't articulate that in words. Not while I watched him devour me, his eyes so hot and hungry as he gazed up at me from between my legs. Not while he ate me like he'd been starved for years.

This man—this gruff, growly man—was on his knees for me, demanding I take every ounce of pleasure from him alone, and the thought had my stomach swooping, my pussy throbbing and aching for relief.

But every time I got close, my orgasm slipped through my fingers like sand. This was always the problem—I got too in my head, thinking about everything else that amounted to absolutely nothing and not being present in the moment. Not enjoying the feel of it, too worried that I didn't look or smell or taste right. That I wasn't making the appropriate amount of noise to show my pleasure, or worse, that I was making too much. That I was taking too long. That he'd get frustrated and—

Beck pulled back and slapped my clit with three fingers, the sharp sting pulling a moan from my throat. "Get out of your head."

"Sorry, I just—"

"No sorries. You see me down on my knees for you, sunshine? I'm going to stay here until I lick up every single drop."

I shuddered at his words, my nipples tightening even further as my pussy throbbed. "But I don't know how long I'll take."

"I don't care."

"But I might—"

He leaned forward and sucked my clit hard into his mouth, tugging a sharp gasp from me. "Sunshine. Are you enjoying this?"

I bit my lip and nodded. Fuck *yes*, I was enjoying this. While my favorite toy branded itself on mimicking oral sex, it had nothing on the real thing. On the wet suction of his mouth, on the targeted flick of his tongue or the sensation of so much happening at once when he added his fingers to the mix.

He reached down and gripped his cock, still thick and hard and straining toward me. "You see this? My cock's so fucking hard because of how good you taste. I could eat you out all damn day, and I'd love every minute of it. Now, keep your eyes on me and watch how much I love devouring this pussy."

Without another word, he dove back in, affixing his mouth to my clit as he curled his fingers inside me, rubbing them against the spot only my vibrators had been able to reach. I gasped, dropping my head back against the tile as he continued whatever magic he was currently working on me. I was primed, my entire body thrumming with need, muscles tightening as I chased the orgasm that was just out of reach.

And then he scraped his teeth over my clit, the jolt of sensation enough to send me careening over the edge. I bowed forward as I came against his mouth, shudders racking my body as his eyes stayed connected with mine. With waves of ecstasy rippling through me, he hummed his satisfaction, working his tongue softly against me to draw out every single ounce of pleasure until I could barely hold myself up.

His gaze was full of hunger as he stood to his full height and boxed me against the wall, his cock so hot and hard between us.

"You taste so fucking good," he said against my lips. Then he kissed me, sweeping his tongue into my mouth so I could taste myself on him.

I groaned, throwing my arms around his neck and pressing my body against his, desperate for more even though I'd just come. I wanted to make him feel as good as he'd done to me. Wanted him inside me, filling me up. Wanted every bit of him he wanted to give.

I lowered one of my hands from around his neck and reached between my legs, rubbing my fingers against my pussy and feeling exactly how much I'd enjoyed having Beck's mouth on me. I gasped against his lips when I brushed my fingers over my sensitive clit, not sure if it was too much or not enough.

"You still need more, baby?" he asked, eyes locked on where my hand disappeared between my legs. "My mouth wasn't enough?"

"This isn't for me," I said and then gripped his thick shaft, using the evidence of my excitement to ease my path as I stroked him.

"Fuck," he breathed, resting his forehead against mine as he stared down to where I pumped his cock. He braced his hands on the wall on either side of my head, caging me in, though there was nowhere in the world I'd rather be than right here, watching him come undone at my touch.

Beck was usually so collected. Stoic and gruff, and it took an act of God to get him excited about something. But right then, he looked so intense, his dark hair hanging over his forehead, lips parted, eyes heavy with lust, and cheeks flushed.

"I want to make you feel good, too." I squeezed his length, tightening my grip enough to pull a grunt from him. "Show me what you like."

CHAPTER ELEVEN

EVERLY

MY WORDS HUNG in the air between us for only a moment before Beck's right hand covered mine and he squeezed on the upstroke, harder than I would've dared, his groan echoing against the tile walls.

"Like that?" I asked, loving that he was taking his pleasure from me. Loving that I was witnessing this part of him.

"Just like that."

"Is this enough?"

"It's never enough with you." He rolled his forehead against mine and closed his eyes as we continued to pump his length. "I want it all—your hands and your mouth and your pussy. Want every fucking inch of you all for myself."

A shiver stole through me at his words, my nipples tight and hard, my body thrumming with desire. I'd never felt this before. Never had this overwhelming need to be with someone, especially after I'd already come. Usually for me, it was one-and-done—actually, it was usually *none*-and-done, and then I had to figure it out for myself after. But with Beck, I felt insatiable, this need building inside me that wasn't satisfied even though he'd just made me see stars.

I pressed up on my toes, my hand still wrapped around his cock, and tugged his bottom lip with my teeth. "I want you to take it."

With a groan, he jerked out of my hand and spun me around, my cheek pressed against the wall, my back presented to him. He ran his hand down my spine, then cupped my ass and squeezed, gripping me harder than I thought I'd like, but I couldn't deny how my pussy throbbed in response. "You can't tell me things like that, baby."

"Why not?" I asked, breathless.

"Because I'll take and take and take."

God, I wanted that. Beck normally gave and gave and gave—in every aspect of his life. He worked long hours, put in extra time, helped out his siblings, fixed things at my house without my even asking. He always did what needed to be done without thought of what he was giving of himself. But here, now...I wanted him to be selfish. I wanted him to be selfish with *me*.

"I want you to. I want you inside me."

"*Fuck*." He slapped his hand on the wall next to my

head, his fingers digging into my ass as he sank his teeth into my neck. "I can't fuck you. Not now. Not like this."

"But I—" My words cut off on a gasp as he shifted forward, sliding his cock through my slit, the head bumping against my clit.

"You need another one, greedy girl?"

"*Yes.*"

"I'm going to take care of you. Put your legs together, baby." He adjusted his stance behind me and squeezed my hips. "Make it nice and tight for me."

I did as he asked, standing on tiptoe and arching my back, presenting my ass to him in hopes that he'd do whatever it was he was planning on because I was dying for more. For his words and his touch. For every bit of him I'd never known before this moment.

And then he gave it to me.

He dragged his erection down the cleft of my ass, bending at the knees so he could slide his cock into the slick, tight space between my legs. I moaned, long and low, as he withdrew and thrust forward again, the thick length of him sliding through my slit, the head of his cock bumping against my clit with each pass.

"*Jesus Christ,*" Beck growled, sinking his teeth into my shoulder as I ached with need, his thrusts picking up speed. "You feel so fucking good, and I'm not even inside you yet. Your pussy's going to ruin me, isn't it, sunshine? Never gonna be the same after I slide inside this tight little cunt."

His words ignited something inside me, the heat building in my core until it felt like every inch of me was a live wire, primed for detonation. I trailed my hand down the front of my body, not stopping until I could feel him sliding through my pussy lips.

"Beck," I breathed, dropping my forehead to the tile, my eyes fluttering closed. I rocked my hips back to meet his thrusts and cupped his pumping cock with my hand, adding more pressure with each pass of it against my clit.

"That's it, baby." He brushed his lips against my shoulder, his fingers digging into my hip as he pressed his other hand on top of mine between my legs. "Use my cock to get yourself off. Show me what you like. Slide that pussy over me and mark me as yours."

Oh *God...* That thought sent a shudder rippling through me. My body was already cresting the wave again, and I couldn't believe it. I'd never in my life come more than once during sex—had never even tried because it'd been such a pipe dream. But the tingle in my limbs and the flutter in my stomach and the throb of my pussy told me that previously unreachable orgasm wasn't far off.

Beck removed his hand from on top of mine, trailing it up my body, between my breasts, until he cupped my throat, and my breath caught. Just last week, I'd flagged a scene like this in the book we were reading. And while it wasn't exactly the same—that had been full-on breath play, where the hero choked the heroine to near unconsciousness as she came—it was still enough to get my attention. Enough to spark my curiosity to try it.

He tightened his fingers, not cutting off my air supply, but enough to be noticed, and my eyes popped open. "What about this? You like my hand on your throat?"

I bit my lip and nodded, my pussy thrumming as I swallowed against the slight pressure from his hand.

"*Fuck*, you're my sweet, greedy girl, aren't you? So desperate to come again." With his fingers still wrapped around my throat, he pressed his thumb to my chin, turning my head toward him so he could capture my mouth in a kiss. He thrust his cock faster against me, his hips slapping my ass as he kissed me and tightened his fingers on my throat.

He was everywhere all at once—pressing me against the shower wall, arms caging me in, fingers wrapped around my neck, body crowding me and making me feel safe and secure and warm. Cared for, even while he used me to get off. While he pumped his cock between my legs, driving us both toward an ecstasy I'd never known.

I was close. So close, so close... And then he squeezed my throat and tugged my nipple just hard enough that a jolt of pain shot through me, and I exploded.

He groaned into my mouth as I came against his cock, his movements growing jerky until he stilled, his hot come spilling out over my hand and my pussy. He kissed me then, a slow, deep slide of his tongue, his hand still cupping my throat, though gentler now, thumb brushing softly along the column of my neck, and I wondered if it could really be this easy. If Beck and I could really become something more.

But a tiny part—the barest whisper in the back of my mind—worried we'd just taken a step we could never come back from.

Beck

I'D JUST COME—*TWICE*—AND my cock was still half hard as I wrapped a towel around myself after handing one to Everly. I wanted to carry her to my room, lay her out on my bed, and spend hours worshipping her body. I wanted to know what every moan, every gasp, every sigh meant and how to elicit them over and over and over again. But I'd already screwed up.

I may not have fucked her in the shower, but I might as well have. I'd spun her around, shoved her into the tile wall, and then jacked myself off against her pussy, all with my hand wrapped around her throat. I'd taken her like she was a one-night stand I didn't care about, instead of one of only two girls in existence I would give the world to. And considering the other was my sister, she didn't count.

I'd used Everly as my own personal sex toy when she deserved to be worshipped.

I could barely look at her, too disgusted with what I'd

done to her to meet her eyes. So instead, I mumbled something about getting dressed and stepped out of the bathroom. I'd barely made it into the main living area when a throat clearing stopped me dead in my tracks.

I snapped my head up, and there my sister stood, leaning back against the counter, not a care in the world.

"How's Everly?" she asked without preamble.

Ford had told me not to worry about opening the diner this morning—that he'd talk to Addison and Aiden and get it taken care of. And with the way Addison's gaze was pinging around the space, it was clear she knew Everly had stayed with me last night and was trying to figure out what was going on between us.

So this was going to be fucking fantastic.

I narrowed my eyes at her, then back to my door that had most definitely been locked. "How'd you get in here?"

She lifted her hand and waved, a key ring with a single key hanging from her middle finger. "Magic."

"I took all your extra keys." After I'd had a close call when she'd nearly walked in on me jacking off—to thoughts of Everly, no doubt—a few months back, I'd ransacked her room at the inn and taken every spare key of mine she'd had—all four of them.

Addison rolled her eyes. "Obviously not."

Before I could respond, Everly strolled out of the bathroom wearing nothing but a towel, and even though it was long on her, it still left little to the imagination. And now, after seeing every inch of her, I'd be able to imagine her in great, Technicolor detail.

I closed my eyes and scrubbed a hand through my hair, preparing myself for Addison's reaction. I had no idea what was going on with Everly and me—if anything would happen beyond what already had—but having my sister walk in on us before we'd managed to discuss any of it between ourselves was about as bad as it could get.

Addison's gaze bounced between Everly and me, her eyes gleaming and looking downright devilish. "*Well...*" she said, dragging out the word.

I stabbed a finger in her direction. "Not one fucking word."

Either my sister was suddenly taking my threats seriously or she was in an exceptionally good mood this morning, because instead of taunting me like I expected, she mimed zipping her lips and tossing away the key.

"Kinda cranky this morning," Everly said. "I figured you'd be in a better mood after...you know."

I snapped my head in her direction, narrowing my eyes, which only pulled a laugh from her.

"Well, I didn't need to hear *that.*" Addison shuddered, then looked at Everly, her eyes heavy with concern. "But apparently my brother is good for something, because you're in better spirits than I thought you'd be."

The smile melted from Everly's face, and she sank into one of the leather chairs, tucking her wet hair behind her ear. "I don't think it's really set in yet, honestly."

"You got out. You got Chuckanut out," Addison said. "That's all that matters."

"Yeah." Everly nodded. "You're right. It could've been worse."

"*So much* worse. Everything else is replaceable."

If my gaze hadn't been glued to Everly, I might have missed the brief flicker of despair that flashed across her face at Addison's words. True, she'd gotten herself and Chuck out, but that home and everything in it were the last things she had of her aunt. The only things that had brought her to Starlight Cove in the first place.

"Yeah," Everly said, her voice scratchy and raw. Her throat was probably still killing her, thanks to the smoke inhalation. Not to mention her reactions in the shower. At least I hadn't shoved my cock down her throat like I'd wanted to. I had something going in my favor.

I gripped my towel—God knew I didn't need a wardrobe malfunction with my sister in the room—as I grabbed Everly another water before thrusting the bottle at her. "Drink."

She glanced up at me, the corner of her mouth tipping up. "Back to single syllables, I see."

Her eyes held a sadness I'd never seen from her before —she could find the silver lining in a hurricane—but even that didn't diminish how gorgeous she was. I scanned her face, cataloguing every inch of her. Drops of water dotted her shoulders, drawing my gaze to the expanse of skin on display, and my cock twitched beneath my towel.

Great. Not only was I getting hard with my sister in the room, but I was doing so as my best friend was reeling from the fire that'd cost her everything. Apparently I'd turned into a fifteen-year-old boy who only cared about his needs and who popped boners thanks to a gust of wind.

Suddenly very aware of the fact that I was standing three feet away from my sister with only a thin piece of terry cloth covering my junk, I twisted back to glare at her. "Why are you still here?"

She rolled her eyes. "That's rude."

"Oh good, then it *is* coming across."

Everly laughed and slapped my leg with the back of her hand. "Don't be mean to your sister."

Addison waved off her concern. "After growing up with these assholes, I learned not to take shit personally."

"Can you take your shit elsewhere, then?"

"Point taken—you don't want me here. Can't imagine why..." She very pointedly glanced between Everly and me, her grin wide.

I blew out a long-suffering sigh. "What the hell do you want, Addison?"

"Right. Well, I had a little break in my schedule, so I came up to see if maybe Everly wanted me to take her shopping to pick up a few things since she..."

Addison let the words trail off, and I slid my gaze to Everly, watching as realization dawned on her face.

Since she didn't have anything left.

When she'd moved to Starlight Cove two years ago, she'd only done so because her aunt had bequeathed her the clinic and attached home. And now, those things were ruined. Who knew if the clinic could be salvaged. If by some miracle, her home was able to be, it would still take substantial remodeling to get it livable again.

Her entire family was clear across the country, and I knew how much she missed them. Washington to her was like Starlight Cove to me. I didn't make sense anywhere else. Would it be worth the effort for her to fix up a home, a business, she hadn't planned on in the first place? To plant roots when she no longer had anything holding her here?

CHAPTER TWELVE

BECK

I SHOULDN'T HAVE WORRIED about hurrying down to the diner after Addison stole Everly away because Ford was having the time of his life. He was made for this job, greeting customers with a smile as he oozed charm, and everyone ate it up. Well, everyone but Quinn Cartwright.

He and the doctor had been oil and water since we were kids, and it hadn't eased any in our adult years. Even when she'd moved back after college and her residency, their friction was still very much alive and well. Though that wasn't too hard to understand. Quinn was always serious, was driven and focused on taking over the town clinic —well, if Dr. Clark ever retired, anyway—and Ford didn't take much of anything seriously, least of all life.

"Well, isn't this a pleasant surprise." He shot Quinn a smile that had most of the women in town melting at his feet. Most, but definitely not her. "Don't usually see you out here."

"I try to avoid it as much as possible." She turned to me. "No offense."

I grabbed a to-go cup and poured her a coffee, the only thing she ever swung in here for. "None taken. I try to avoid him as much as possible, too."

Ford snorted. "Sure, Doc. Whatever you say. I just think it's convenient, is all."

She blew out a long sigh and hung her head. "I'm going to regret this, but what's convenient?"

He shrugged. "You obviously figured I'd be working in here today after the night Beck had, so you had to swing by. But don't worry. Your secret's safe with me."

She just stared at him blankly, not taking the bait, and sipped her coffee. Then she dismissed him completely without a word and turned to me. "How's Everly doing?"

I opened my mouth to respond and realized I couldn't answer the question because...I didn't know. Sure, I'd given Everly two orgasms before breakfast, so it wasn't all bad, but I hadn't even asked her how she'd been feeling this morning. Hadn't asked her if her throat was sore, if she was hungry, if her hands hurt from the scrapes.

The only thing I'd done to even acknowledge the fact that she'd been in a fire last night was shove a water bottle in her face when her voice got scratchy and demand she drink. *A+ behavior, asshole.*

I cleared my throat. "As good as can be expected."

Quinn's eyes softened, nothing like the daggers she'd been shooting Ford's way. "I can't imagine how difficult this is for her. But let her know she can call me anytime if she has any questions or concerns or is just feeling off."

"What?" I snapped my gaze to hers. "Why would she be feeling off? Is there something I should be looking for?"

Quinn huffed out a laugh and shook her head. "No, nothing like that. Just...if she needs someone to talk to, I'm around."

My brows drew down, but I gave her a short nod, trying to hide how much I hated the thought of Everly seeking comfort from someone other than me. "Right. Sure."

"Well, I need to head out." She dropped some cash on the counter and held up her coffee. "Thanks for this."

"I'll text you my schedule for the coming week," Ford called after her retreating form. "So you know where to find me."

Her gaze was cool and disinterested as she stared back at him, but her middle finger twitched on her cup. I'd bet all the money in the register that if there weren't other people in here and she weren't vying for the town physician role and needed to play a part, she would've sent him a one-finger salute as she marched her ass out of the diner.

"Smooth," I said to Ford as the door closed behind her.

He snorted. "I wasn't trying to be smooth. Believe me, if I laid on the charm, she'd be putty in my hands. But why should I waste the good stuff on her?"

"Uh-huh."

"No, seriously, I could—"

"Take care of the tables outside? Just what I was thinking." With a hard push to his shoulder, I shoved him in that direction.

He laughed and grabbed a pitcher of water before heading outside. Chuckanut was out there, her leash long enough for her to roam freely. And actually, maybe it was *her* I needed to have here greeting people every morning, because the customers ate it up. How Everly's sunshine persona had morphed into a dog, too, I'd never know, but there was no denying it. Chuckanut trotted from table to table with an honest to God smile, soaking in all the attention, and the diners seemed to love it.

Ford topped off her water dish, then made the rounds outside while I took care of the customers in here, thankfully busy enough that I was constantly moving and couldn't focus on the niggle in the back of my mind that said I'd screwed up with Everly this morning. That I'd been too demanding, too pushy, too *much*. That I'd taken our relationship somewhere she'd never intended it to go. Somewhere we couldn't come back from.

But she'd been with me, hadn't she? She'd been moaning my name, coming over my tongue and my cock. She'd sought my embrace before she'd left with Addison, pressing a kiss to the underside of my jaw like everything was business as usual.

Well, business as usual except for the fact that I now

knew what her pussy tasted like and that she liked a little pain mixed with her pleasure to get off...

A couple hours later, when the last person finally cleared out of the diner, Ford strolled in, Chuck trotting along at his heels.

He slid onto a stool at the bar and braced his elbows on the counter. "Jesusfuck, I thought they'd never leave."

"Who?"

He gestured behind him. "The couple visiting from Ohio."

I stared at him blankly. "*You* kept them here talking for the past fifteen minutes."

"Well, what was I supposed to do? We can't all grunt and throw food at people."

"I didn't throw food at anyone today." Even though there'd been a few who absolutely deserved it.

"Quit distracting me," he said. "I need to know how it was."

I glanced at him with a raised brow as I wiped down the counter. "How what was?"

"The sex, obviously."

I paused for only half a second, arm outstretched, before I kept right on with the rag, hoping he hadn't noticed. "I never said I had sex."

He snorted and shot Chuck a look that said *can you believe this guy*. "You didn't have to. I can just tell."

"I'm calling bullshit on that. I can't tell when *you* have sex."

"You can't tell because this is my baseline," he said, circling his face. "But you, my friend, have been stagnant for, what? Two years? Believe me, there's a difference."

I glared at him for several seconds, hoping he'd back down, but he just stared back, grin on his face, and waited for me to crack.

"Fuck," I snapped, slapping the rag down on the counter.

"*Yes.*" He fist-pumped the air. "Fuck is right."

"You're a jackass. I mean fuck, as in *fuck me*. Fuck, as in I fucked up. Fuck, as in I don't know what the fuck I was thinking."

"Well, you were probably thinking Everly's hot and amazing and is open-minded as hell in bed if those books she reads are anything to go by—not to mention the highlighted parts. *Jesus.*"

"How did you—"

"And her ass looks fantastic in jeans—"

"Hey," I barked.

"Plus, you've been in love with her for two years—"

"I am not in lo—"

"And have basically declared your complete and utter devotion to her anyway since you haven't been with anyone since she so much as stepped foot into town, so you might as well have sex while you're at it."

"We didn't have sex," I bit out through clenched teeth. When he just raised a brow, I groaned and pulled off my hat, running a frustrated hand through my hair before replacing it. "*Technically*, we didn't, but I still fucked up. I can't believe I did that."

"Yeah, I'm pretty shocked too. At this point, I figured it'd take an act of God to get you to cross that boundary. Nice job."

"*Nice job*? Are you serious? I'm worried about ruining the best relationship I've ever had, and you want to pat me on the back?"

"Um, first of all, hello?" He reached over and flicked me on the forehead. "*I'm* the best relationship you've ever had."

"You don't count."

"And second, you didn't ruin it."

"You can't know that."

"Well, you can't know you did, either. Did she *say* you ruined it?"

"No."

"Did she act any differently?"

I assumed he probably didn't mean differently in the way that I now knew what she sounded like when she came and that her blush did, in fact, spread down her chest when she was turned on. "No."

He shrugged. "Then you didn't ruin it."

"It's not always that simple."

"Sometimes it is," Ford said, all notes of teasing gone.

"Aren't you always the one reminding me I have a one hundred percent fail rate at relationships?"

"*Everyone* has a one hundred percent fail rate at relationships unless they're currently in a committed relationship. And nobody involved in this conversation is. That doesn't mean you just give up entirely. What, are you going to spend the rest of your life alone?"

"Since you're always up my ass, that'd be impossible."

"Maybe now, but one of these days, I'm going to lock down a cool-as-fuck woman, have her make an honest man out of me, and enjoy the hell out of making some babies with her. And then where are you going to be?"

"Oh, you think *you're* going to be able to make a relationship last? We grew up in the same house with the same parents. And our examples weren't exactly shining."

Yes, our mom had been an amazing mother who loved her family beyond all reason. She strived for perfection, but that had been hard, considering she was basically a single parent raising six kids. It didn't matter that she was technically married and that our dad was technically around. Not when he chose alcohol over her and us time and time again. She'd tried to keep that hidden from us, but the older we'd gotten, the easier it had been to see. There'd been fights and makeups and so much tension it was like a constant weight bearing down on us.

If that was what love was—what forever was—I didn't want any part of it.

"Brady had the same parents, too," Ford said, pulling a piece of bacon from God knew where and feeding it to Chuck. "You don't think he and Luna are going to last?"

Truthfully, I didn't know. I hoped they would because he deserved it after stepping in as the family leader and pulling us through years of struggles without so much as a single complaint. And Luna was good for him, softening his sharp edges and loosening him up a bit. But I couldn't see the future for them any more than I could see it for myself.

"Look, man, nobody knows what's going to happen tomorrow, let alone in years," he said. "Our family is aware of that more than most. But what I *do* know is that you'd rather cut off your own balls than hurt Everly."

I blew out a breath, wanting his words to ring true but unable to deny the reality. "I might have already hurt her, though."

He squinted one eye and tipped his head to the side, studying me. "Nah, I don't think so. I saw her this morning, and for someone whose house just burned down, she was in a better mood than I expected. I'm guessing that had something to do with your *technically not sex*. You take note of those highlighted parts too and use them to your advantage?"

"How the hell do you know about those?"

He shrugged. "She left a book sitting on the counter one day. I peeked. And got a whole fucking eyeful."

I jabbed a finger in his direction. "Erase that knowledge from your brain right fucking now."

He grinned, just a flash of teeth before he sobered again, bracing his elbows on the counter as he leaned toward me. "Look, just keep doing what you're doing, and don't overthink it."

Yeah. Great. *Don't overthink it.* Overthinking might as well have been my middle name.

"Right," he said with a laugh. "Forgot who I was talking to for a minute. That's pretty much like telling Oscar the Grouch to stop grouching. I guess that means you're going to have to talk to her about it. You guys talk about everything else—including your kink of the week—so this should be child's play."

I could only hope he was right and that we'd figure this out like we'd figured everything else out thus far. I should've talked to her before she left, though my pain-in-the-ass sister had made that impossible. Then again, Everly had so much else to deal with right now, the last thing she needed piled on her shoulders was this.

Chuck let out the softest bark known to man as she sat dutifully at Ford's feet, tongue hanging out of her mouth, which made it look like she was grinning, and he fed her another piece of bacon.

"Where the hell are you getting that bacon from?" I asked.

"Got a whole pocket full of it."

"Jesus. No wonder she was following you around out there."

He grinned. "Women love a man with a dog."

"She's not your dog."

"Doesn't matter."

I blew out a breath and shook my head. "You know grease stains are a bitch to get out, right?"

"They're in a baggie. I'm not a Neanderthal."

"I'm not so sure. And I bet I could get Quinn to back me up on that."

He rolled his eyes. "Like I'm going to put any stock in what she thinks of me. That woman wouldn't know a good time if it slapped her on the ass and handcuffed her to a bed."

"Thought about that a time or two, have you?"

He avoided the question entirely and instead asked, "What time are Addison and Everly supposed to be back?"

They'd already been gone for hours, and I was about ready to call Addison and tell her to get her ass back here. "No idea, but knowing our sister, she's keeping Everly out extra long just to piss me off."

"Sounds about right." He glanced at the clock on the wall, then back to me with a raised brow, chin jutting toward the bags we'd stashed behind the counter. "You want to do this when Everly gets back?"

I was shaking my head before he even got the question out. "Nope."

She might know about Ford's and my weekly excursions, but she didn't have to witness them. My luck, that'd be the one time the bastard would answer the door.

"Then it's now or never, I guess."

With a nod, I picked up the bag I'd already packed full of three oversized meals that could be stretched out to six or seven, and Ford grabbed a couple books he'd picked up from the library. Then we headed out of the diner, Chuck at our heels.

She trotted along beside us, no leash needed, as we walked the same path we'd walked every Wednesday for the past almost ten years when Ford and I visited our father. Okay, *visited* was a gross overstatement of what we really did, which was drop off some food and a few books on his front porch without even knocking.

To be fair, we *had* knocked. For months. And still never got a response, not even in the early days right after Mom had died. We assumed because there wasn't a horrible stench coming from the cottage or flies incessantly buzzing around that he hadn't joined her. That was probably a detached way to talk about our own father, but it was only a reflection of what he'd given us.

Over the years, I'd seen all my siblings—save for Levi —come and go from Cottage Thirteen. Brady dropped off groceries once a week, Addison took care of the property, and Aiden swapped out Dad's linens, though none of them knew I knew, like they were ashamed or embarrassed about it, and I could understand why. None of them knew Ford and I made this stop every week, either, and I'd prefer to keep it that way. It was hard enough for me to reconcile wanting to make sure the father who'd abandoned his kids was still taken care of, while being furious at him over his choices.

The older I got, the more of him I saw in myself. We

had the same outlook, the same surly temperament, the same off-putting nature. While I'd picked up Mom's love for cooking, I was basically a carbon copy of my dad, and I hated it.

After Mom had died, he might as well have, too, leaving all six of us to fend for ourselves. Addison hadn't even been eighteen yet, and we'd all had to step in and fill the role of her parent. Because one had left us by circumstances beyond her control, and the other had left us by choice because he felt like he had nothing left to live for. Even if he still had us.

I was terrified to follow in his footsteps, loving someone completely, only to have them leave in the end, because I'd already been there. My parents had both shown me love wasn't truly unconditional. And it sure as hell wasn't meant to last.

CHAPTER THIRTEEN

EVERLY

THANKFULLY, Addison and I were within half a shoe size of each other, so I was able to borrow a pair of hers for our shopping excursion to replenish my necessities. And Luna, Brady's girlfriend, had sent over some clothes with Addison since we were about the same size. I'd slipped into a pair of her leggings but opted to wear one of Beck's T-shirts instead of any she'd offered. I wasn't too proud to admit the flimsy piece of cotton comforted me in a way I needed as I went out on a mission in borrowed clothes to replace my belongings.

Also thankfully, Addison was like a tornado. She flew through stores, barking orders and making demands, and because she was Starlight Cove's golden child and she gave those orders with a smile, people willingly did her bidding. I had no idea how she did it. I felt like I was still trying to win people over in town, even after two years, and that was with an always-ready smile. But regardless of how she did it, I was grateful for her.

I was grateful for a lot of things today—that I'd escaped from the fire, that Chuckanut had made it out with me, and that neither of us had any lasting injuries. I was also overwhelmingly grateful for Beck—Beck's whole family, actually, but him specifically.

Before Addison and I had left, I'd realized I didn't have my purse, which meant I didn't have any money or even a credit card to pay for what I needed, and I'd panicked. As usual, Beck had immediately read me without my having to say a word. With his eyes locked on mine, he'd pulled out his wallet, handed his credit card to Addison, and then said, just loud enough for me to hear, "Whatever you need."

And then, as if to balance things out and prove he wasn't a gigantic marshmallow, he'd thrust a bottle of water at me as Addison and I were walking out the door and yelled after us, "And don't forget to eat, for fuck's sake!"

Addison had rolled her eyes, but I'd smiled, so relieved that the Beck I knew and loved was still there, despite what had happened between us. It hadn't changed us—I just had to remember that. He was still my best friend. Still my touch point in Starlight Cove. And no matter what happened, I didn't want to lose that.

Now, Addison pulled up in front of our last stop and parked. Main Street was fairly busy today even though it was the middle of the week, no doubt because it was a beautiful day. That meant plenty of people strolled by, and every single one wanted to stop us and tell me how shocked they were to hear what had happened and ask if I was okay. Every time, I'd plaster a smile on my face and pretend like I wasn't completely crumbling inside at having to relive it with every mention.

"Last one," Addison said, grabbing her purse.

"Oh, thank God." My shoulders slumped. "I don't think I can take much more."

She reached over and rested her hand on my arm, stopping me from unbuckling my seat belt. "Why don't you sit this one out? I've got it."

I blew out a huge sigh of relief and shot her a grateful smile. Apparently, Addison was as perceptive as her brother. Either that or I looked every ounce as exhausted as I felt. It took a lot for me to break, but after recounting the worst night of my life over and over and over again, I was ready to crack.

All the small—and not-so-small things—that needed to be done had also started piling up in my mind, and I'd been keeping a mental tally of everything I needed to do as we were running around replacing all my possessions. Luckily, I'd had a voice mail waiting for me this morning from April, my assistant-slash-receptionist, saying she'd seen the news—on Facebook, naturally—and that she'd take care of rescheduling our appointments until we knew more.

Like, if I still had a business or not.

"Thank you," I said earnestly to Addison as I grabbed my phone from where I'd stashed it in the cupholder. "I still need to call my parents and let them know what happened."

Addison grimaced. "Will that be an easy or a difficult call?"

I must not have been able to keep the cringe to myself, because she nodded without my having to say a word.

"Got it. In that case, I think I'll swing by the bakery to grab two donuts. Maybe three..."

"Is that for just me or both of us?"

Addison gasped and snapped her head in my direction. "Both of us, obviously. I deserve donuts too."

I laughed. "You definitely do, but in that case, make it four."

Her smile widened as she opened the door and stepped out. "I like how you think."

As she strode toward the sidewalk, dodging passersby like she was on an obstacle course, I lowered my gaze to my phone and pulled up my mom's number—it took an act of God for my dad to answer his phone, mostly because he could never find the thing. And if he could find it, he couldn't figure out how to use it.

I'd been putting this off all day, but I couldn't wait any longer. I took a deep breath and exhaled slowly as I pressed the call button.

After one and a half rings, my mom answered, "Honey! I wasn't expecting to hear from you today. Don't tell me I got my days wrong again. Is it Sunday already? You know how it is with retirement."

"I know, Mom. All the days bleed together," I said, reciting the same phrase she'd said to me no fewer than twelve thousand times. "And no, it's not Sunday. It's Wednesday, but I have something important I need to tell you. Is Dad around?"

"Oh yes, he's just tinkering with his model cars. I'll grab him." She moved the phone away from her mouth but not far enough that it saved me from the earsplitting yell as she called for him. "Harry! Evie's on the phone. She's got something to tell us." Then, quieter but still loud enough for me to hear, she said, "Maybe she's finally moving home!"

I closed my eyes, knowing that last night's catastrophe was only going to embolden them further in their quest to get me back to the West Coast, and I wasn't sure I was up for that particular confrontation today. Honestly, I was never up for that particular confrontation, which was probably why my stomach churned every Sunday until I got our weekly call over with.

"Okay, honey, your dad's right next to me. Are you still there?"

"I'm here. Hey, Dad."

"Hi, angel. So, what's this all about?"

"Some exciting news, perhaps?" my mom said, her smile carrying through in her voice.

"Well, I wouldn't exactly call it exciting. But news? Yes."

I cleared my throat, wincing at the sting, and closed my eyes, knowing it was best to rip it off like a bandage. "Aunt Shirley's house caught on fire last night."

As predicted, my mom gasped loudly enough that the neighbors probably heard her, and my dad said, "What'd she say? Did she say there was a fire?"

"Oh my heavens. Are you okay?" Mom's voice rose with every word. "What happened? Did Chuckanut make it out? Where are you staying?"

"One at a time, Mom."

She expelled a deep breath, then asked, "Chuckanut?"

"She's fine." I'd only seen her briefly when Addison and I had left. She'd been soaking up the sun and the attention of everyone on the diner's patio, so she barely paid me any mind when I'd buried my face in her neck and squeezed, realizing that Ford was an absolute saint. Not only had he watched her for me last night when I couldn't take her with me to the hospital, but he'd also bathed her so only the faint hint of smoke lingered.

"And you?" Mom asked, her voice shaking. "Are you okay, honey?"

"I'm fine, too, Mom," I said, but my voice cracked, and she heard right through it.

I wouldn't call losing my home—and possibly my business—being *fine*, but what else could I be?

"Oh, honey, I know this must be so awful for you." She tutted. "But maybe it's for the best."

I sucked in a sharp breath, blinking through the shock

of what she'd just said, the crack in my chest growing a bit wider at her words. While I knew she didn't mean for them to come off as dismissive, that was exactly how they had. I definitely got my sunny disposition from her, but there was such a thing as toxic positivity, and my mom was teeming with it. Sometimes when catastrophe struck, people didn't want to hear that everything happened for a reason or that maybe it was for the best. No, maybe it just sucked ass.

"That didn't come out how I meant it," she said. "I just mean that now you have nothing left. Nothing holding you there."

I huffed out a disbelieving laugh and shook my head, so tired of having this conversation with her. Without fail, she'd mention it every single week on our phone calls, and every week, I felt like I was disappointing them over and over again by not going home. But by going home, I'd feel like I was disappointing Aunt Shirley. I couldn't win.

"Except for the life I've built here over the past couple years," I said.

My mom huffed, her disapproval loud and clear. "Oh, your brother told us all about that *life*. I didn't realize that fellow you've been telling us all about was such a..." She sniffed. "Well, I'm not going to repeat the word your brother called him, but I'm sure you can use your imagination."

I closed my eyes and dropped my head back against the seat. Of *course* Ash would report back to my parents about his encounter with Beck and then scurry off to

Jamaica like the coward he was so I couldn't lay into him. "Well, did he also tell you that the reason they even spoke was because Beck was at my house, fixing the things I tried to pay someone else to do? Or that the only way I remember to eat half the time is because he makes sure I do, even when I'm swamped? Or that he's the one person here who's made this place feel like home?"

My mom tsked. "Oh, honey. If he's really the only person who's made Starlight Cove feel like home, isn't that more proof that you don't belong there? You belong home, *here*, with us. With your family. The people who will love and support you through this while you figure out what you want to do next."

And that was the kicker—I didn't know what I wanted to do next. I'd crafted a life based on other people's expectations—from my love for animals that had bloomed because my parents sent me to stay with my aunt over the summers, to the school I chose on the West Coast to stay close to family. Even moving to Starlight Cove had been because someone else had made the decision for me, and I'd done what was expected.

Who even was I without everyone else's expectations tied to me like strings?

While my mom's intentions were pure—she just wanted me closer because she loved me—I knew what would happen if I went back home, because it was the same thing that always happened. I'd do what they thought I should, with little to no regard or care as to if *I* actually wanted to, because that was who I was. A people pleaser to my core, especially when it came to my parents. Yes, I was thirty years old, and yes, it was ridiculous, but it was what it was. And at least I was aware of it enough now to be able to avoid it.

But I wouldn't be able to avoid it forever.

Addison opened the car door and slid into her seat, holding up a large bakery bag and shooting me a grin. I tried to smile back, but it must have come off more like a grimace because her eyes softened.

Before I could tell my mom—once again—I wasn't planning on moving back to Washington, she cut in, "So, when's your flight back?" And the hopeful note in her voice dropped another boulder into my already churning stomach.

"Mom," I said softly, shifting my attention out the passenger window. "I'm not moving back home."

"Right *now*, you mean."

No, I meant I wasn't moving home, period, but I couldn't handle opening up that can of worms and dealing with the fallout of that conversation after everything else. I thought that my moving here, thousands of miles away, meant I'd get a reprieve from that ever-present pit in my stomach over the thought of disappointing my parents. But it'd somehow gotten worse, the guilt like an unwanted houseguest who just wouldn't leave.

So instead of correcting her and reiterating my stance, I just said, "Right. Not right now."

"Well, your old room is here and ready for you whenever you come back, angel," my dad said, loud enough to be heard over a freight train, and I pulled my phone away from my ear with a cringe. I'd tried to tell him a hundred times he didn't need to yell if they were on speakerphone, but it never seemed to get through.

"Great, thank you," I said, desperate to end the call. "I have to go—my phone's about to die. But I'll call you both on Sunday. Love you."

I didn't wait to hear their responses before I ended the call and dropped my phone back into the cupholder.

"Since your battery says it's at seventy-two percent, I'm going to go out on a limb and guess you're having parent woes," Addison said.

"Something like that."

"You want to talk about it? I'm no Beck, but I won't growl or bark at you, so that's something."

I huffed out a laugh before the smile slowly slipped from my mouth. "They just haven't accepted that I live here. And now, after the fire, they're assuming I'm moving back."

Addison's brows lifted. "Are you?"

"No!" The answer came out automatically, but as she stared at me, clearly trying to gauge if I was leaving something unsaid, I wondered if that was true.

My mom had a point—my family *was* three thousand miles away. The only person I'd made a solid connection with in this town was Beck, and who knew if what had happened this morning would screw that up. Even though I'd been here for years, I still didn't quite feel like I fit.

But I also didn't want to leave.

I'd loved this town since I was a little girl. I loved the festivals and the colorful residents. I loved that I didn't have to lock my doors and could walk on the beach at midnight if I wanted to. I loved that the people here looked out for their own. Case in point, the bags currently filling up the back seat of Addison's car with very little use of Beck's credit card.

But were those reasons enough for me to stay?

CHAPTER FOURTEEN

EVERLY

THE DINER CLOSED early on Wednesdays, so there were no customers to contend with when Addison dropped me off before heading to the main inn. The resort was busier than I'd ever seen it, and several guests strolled along the shore and walked the winding path through the cottages. I was thrilled for Beck and his family that the resort had had a bit of a break after several years of barely getting by. They deserved it.

There was no place in Starlight Cove that made me feel as content as this place did. It was why I ran here instead of around town. It was quiet enough to think and so peaceful, it was hard not to feel at home.

I turned, ready to gather my things and head up to Beck's apartment, but I did a double take when I saw Mabel—an older resident and Starlight Cove's self-proclaimed investigative reporter, always ready at the scene to get the scoop for her infamous Facebook Lives—hiding in the bushes behind the diner.

With raised brows, I lifted a hand to wave, but she ducked farther into the brush, as if even the thickest foliage would've been able to hide her in all her fuchsia jogging suit glory.

I shook my head and reached for my bags, but before I could get far, Chief Brambert pulled up in front of the diner. He was a nice, if gruff, older man, probably around my dad's age, with dark skin and a thick beard but not a hair on his head. After I'd performed emergency surgery on his dog, Martha, shortly after I'd moved here, he'd been nothing but kind to me. But my stomach still bottomed out at the sight of him.

He stepped out of his truck, still wearing his uniform. "Hey there, kiddo."

"Hey, Chief Brambert," I said, trying to hide the slight shake in my voice over the fact that this man was about to reveal my future.

"Aw, come on now, Everly. You know it's just Jim."

"Okay, Jim. Did you..." I swallowed down my apprehension over what his answer might be and asked, "Have you been to my house?"

"Yeah. That's why I'm here. I was going to give you a call but thought this might warrant an in-person chat. Talked to Jana down at the bakery, who said you're staying out here."

I flattened my lips together and nodded, my nails

pressing crescent moons into my arms from where they were crossed over my chest. "Yeah. With Beck."

"Good. That's real good. I'm glad you've got a place to stay because... Well, there's no easy way to say this—"

"Hang on just a minute, Chief!" Mabel called, shuffling in our direction as fast as her short legs would carry her, her phone pointed toward us. "Want to be sure I catch all of this for the Live..."

"Mabel, I'm not sure now's the time for this," Jim said.

"Oh, nonsense." Mabel swatted her hand through the air. "The residents need to know if we've got an arsonist on the loose, setting fires and burning down beautiful, much-needed businesses. And the historical home!" She pressed a hand to her chest. "Oh, I can't even believe someone would set it on fire. And while Everly and her sweet dog were inside!"

"Now, wait just a minute. I never said—"

"You hush now, Chief. Besides, Everly doesn't mind if I record this." She turned to me, phone pointed in my direction. "Do you, sugar?"

Actually, I did kind of mind—this wasn't exactly what I'd like splashed all over Starlight Cove's Facebook page—but now wasn't the time to stand my ground. So instead, I gave her a tight smile and directed my attention back to the chief. "It's fine, Jim. What's the news?"

He nodded, tucking his hands into his pockets. "Well, it looks like it started in your kitchen—faulty outlet. The residence portion of the structure is severely damaged—

that's no surprise. And though the crew was able to contain the fire before it could engulf the clinic like it did the living quarters, I'm afraid that portion still sustained too much damage to be safe."

The words sank in, confirming the worst outcome, and I closed my eyes. Everything I had here in Starlight Cove was gone. *Poof*. Just like that. And it'd happened in a matter of four and a half minutes—thankfully not because of a candle I'd left burning, which had niggled at the back of my mind. But now, I had no house, no furniture, no business.

I had nothing.

Tears pricked the backs of my eyes, and I swallowed repeatedly, trying to force them down. I didn't want to cry out here, in front of Jim and Mabel, not to mention who knew how many people watching the Live. But I didn't know how long I'd be able to hold it in. I just wished there wasn't going to be a front-row seat to my impending breakdown.

"You saw it here first, folks," Mabel cut in, standing in front of me while holding her phone toward us. "I'm down at Starlight Cove Resort in front of the diner, where Chief Brambert just delivered Everly Bowman—owner of the totally and completely burned to a crisp veterinary clinic —the worst news possible. As you can see, she's taking this *exceptionally* hard, though I would be, too, if everything I had was suddenly—"

"Mabel!"

At the sound of Beck's sharp bark, both the chief and Mabel startled, but I relaxed, my shoulders sagging in relief. How he knew I needed him now more than ever, I had no idea, but he was just the distraction I required. He stormed down the stairs, the picture of masculinity with his thick thighs encased in worn denim, his broad, muscular chest and shoulders outlined almost pornographically by a standard white T-shirt, and a backward baseball hat hiding a lush head of hair. And then to top off all that hotness, he carried Chuckanut under his arm like a football while she smiled the whole way.

His eyes were dark and laser focused as he stormed toward us. No...toward *Mabel*. "What the hell are you doing?" Without waiting for her to answer, he plucked her phone right out of her hand, shut it off, and dropped it into his pocket.

"Hey!" she said, hands on hips. "You can't keep that! I'm just doing my civic duty and keeping residents informed."

"What you're doing is being a menace."

"You say that like it's a bad thing."

Beck pressed his lips into a flat line and pointed his finger in the direction of where she'd parked her scooter. "Go home."

"But my phone!"

"Starlight Cove's had enough of your so-called news for the night. You can come back and pick it up in the morning. Or you can stand here and keep pissing me off, and I'll throw it in the ocean instead."

"You wouldn't!"

"Try me," he snapped. "Now get out of here."

Mabel sniffed, attempting to look imposing as she stood toe-to-toe with Beck, hands on hips as she glared up at him. "Or what?"

"Or I'll call Brady. He's arrested his girlfriend plenty, so I don't think he'll have a problem arresting you."

She blew out a raspberry. "Between you, Brady, and Aiden, I never get to have any fun. Why can't I ever get stuck with the entertaining McKenzie brothers?"

"Happy to send Ford your way," Beck grumbled to her back as she walked toward her scooter.

Chief Brambert cleared his throat. "I really do wish I had better news to give you, kiddo."

I nodded, unable to find my words. Unable to think about anything but the bomb he'd just dropped. That interaction between Beck and Mabel had been a nice little distraction, but just as quickly, everything came rushing back, and I leaned into Beck, my mind a whir of chaos over what I was going to do now.

———

SOMEHOW, in the midst of my major panic, Beck finished up with the chief, then guided me upstairs, hauling all my purchases as well as Chuckanut, while I could barely manage the steps on my own.

He set her down as soon as we stepped inside, then pointed to a chair. "Sit."

Chuckanut did his bidding, but I knew he wasn't talking to her. We were back to single syllables again, and I wasn't even up for giving him shit about it, so I did as he said, shuffling over before dropping into the chair we'd slept in last night.

Beck opened his fridge and pulled out the bottle of wine I'd opened two days ago—before the fire, before my life was nothing but ashes—and poured me a healthy glass, all while keeping his eyes locked on me. Then, he opened the cupboard above his fridge and pulled down a bowl of Starbursts—the FaveReds version because why would you choose any other flavors?—and brought both over.

He squatted in front of me, setting the candy on the table and holding the glass out to me, his hand resting on my thigh. "Tell me what happened."

I grabbed the glass, taking a large swallow, unable to look away from his piercing gaze. "Well, my house is ruined, and the clinic is unusable. Which means I don't know what I'm going to do. Just because I don't have a working clinic anymore doesn't mean animals stop needing care. April canceled twelve appointments from this week alone! There're still all the appointments that are already on the books. Besides figuring out all that, I also need to deal with insurance, I have to replace my driver's license, call all my credit card companies and get replacements—but first, I need to make a list of all the cards I had. God, I don't even remember half of them." A hysterical laugh bubbled free, and I swallowed another gulp of wine. "And it feels like things are weird between us after last night and then the shower, and I hate that. Oh, and I still need to check in and get a cottage, though I don't have a reservation, so—"

"Not happening," he said sharply.

"What?"

He blew out a long breath. "The resort's booked through June."

I stared at him for three seconds and then promptly burst into tears. Everything I'd been suppressing came pouring out of me, and all I could do was allow it to. I didn't often have a soul-baring cry, but when I finally reached the point of this level of tears, there was no holding them back. No minimizing or containing them. It was like a waterfall on my face.

Beck's eyes widened the tiniest fraction, and even through my tears, I could see the panic written on his features. He made a gruff sound in the back of his throat, set my glass on the table, and then scooped me into his arms. He flipped our places, sitting down in the chair with me draped over his lap.

He held me as I soaked his shirt with my tears, his arms banded around me so tightly I couldn't feel anything but safe and secure. Just like I'd felt in the shower when he'd been surrounding me, his body blanketing mine.

Just like I'd felt last night before the kiss and in the ambulance when he'd found me. Just like I always felt with him.

"You're staying here," he said, his lips barely moving from where they rested against my forehead.

I sniffed, tipping my head back to look up at him, tears still pooling in my eyes. "What?"

He reached up, swiping away my tears with his thumb, though it was no use because more just followed. "The resort's full, but it wouldn't matter if it weren't because you're not staying there. You're staying *here*."

"But you only have one bedroom," I said like he hadn't seen me naked just hours before.

"Sunshine," he said, his voice just a low rumble. "I came all over your pussy this morning. I think we can probably share a bed."

"Beck..." I bit my lip, my memories of what'd happened slamming into me and effectively taking my mind off the clusterfuck that was my life. "We should probably talk about that, too."

"Will it stop you from crying?"

"Maybe?" It would certainly help to focus my attention elsewhere.

"Fine. Great. Let's talk about it, then."

I breathed out a watery laugh. "I know we didn't have sex, but you"—I gestured with my hands as if that could encompass what I meant—"all over my, you know..."

"We've established that."

"Well, we haven't established if we're, you know, being safe."

"Why would we need to establish it? You just got your IUD replaced last month."

I should've probably remembered he knew that, considering he'd glowered at me the whole night while aggressively feeding me grilled cheese and pain relievers. "Pregnancy isn't the only thing to worry about, you know."

He furrowed his brow, his eyes hard. "You think I would've done that with you if I weren't completely sure I was safe?"

I blew out a long exhale and shook my head. Beck would rather cut off his own dick than put me in danger, regardless if we were talking about life and death or a paper cut. "Well, I'm clear, too."

"I figured since the asshat staying at your house was your brother."

"He's not—"

"And I don't want things to be weird between us."

I sagged against him and shook my head. "I don't either."

"Then they're not," he said with finality, like his word was law.

Considering how stubborn he was, it didn't seem entirely implausible. And I was just going to roll with it because it was one less thing I needed to worry about.

"So, we're good?"

He pressed a kiss to my forehead. "We're good."

"Good, then give me something else to think about. Tell me about your day. What were you doing before I came home?"

Something flared in his eyes, but it was gone before I could identify it. "Cooking Chuck dinner."

"Her name is *Chuckanut*—"

"Dumbest name I've ever heard," he grumbled under his breath.

"And I bought her food." I tipped my chin toward the bags he'd carried up. "You don't have to make anything for her."

He scoffed. "You call that dry garbage you buy in bulk *food*? You're not feeding her that shit anymore."

"Beck." I rubbed my eyes, scrubbing away the last of my tears, both grateful that he'd been able to shift my mood so quickly and exasperated with him all over again. "It's not shit. I'm a vet, and I promise you I'm not feeding her garbage."

He stared down at me, brow raised. "Are you feeding her fresh, all-organic ingredients?"

"Well...no."

"Then it's garbage."

I breathed out a laugh and shook my head, more grateful for him than I could possibly articulate, but I needed to try. "Thank you."

"For what?"

"For taking care of me and Chuckanut and letting us stay here and paying for everything today—I'll pay you back as soon as I get my replacement cards—and knowing that I needed wine and Starbursts without my saying a word."

"You don't have to thank me for any of that."

"No, I do. And I need to—" I gasped, suddenly realizing what day it was, and sat up straight, darting my eyes all over his face to gauge his mood. "It's Wednesday! Are you okay?"

Probably an odd question since I was the one with tear tracks down their face, but a fair one, nonetheless. When I'd first arrived in Starlight Cove, he'd kept to himself on Wednesdays—always closed off in the mornings and never anywhere to be found the rest of the day. At least until I'd accidentally run into him one week. He'd been grumpier than usual, so I'd dragged him up to his apartment and forced him to watch *House Hunters: Comedians on Couches* with me because I figured he'd enjoy how they completely roasted the couples.

That'd been the start of our Wednesday ritual, and it had continued every week since. But it hadn't been until a few months ago that he'd actually told me *why* he was always in such a foul mood on those days. He hadn't had to swear me to secrecy—that was an unspoken agreement regarding everything in our friendship and something I'd just known from how he held things so close to his chest—but we hadn't really talked about it since. I only knew that he and Ford dropped some things off for their dad—who, apparently, lived on the property, but whom I'd never once seen in my two years in Starlight Cove.

Beck made a gruff sound in the back of his throat, his eyes scanning my features as if to make sure I wasn't about to have another breakdown. "Don't worry about me."

"But worrying about you takes my mind off all the things I should be worrying about for *me*."

"Let me worry about all the things for you, all right?" Before I could answer, he stood with me still in his arms.

"What are we doing?"

"*We* are going to sit outside on the roof, listen to the ocean, and stare up at the stars. *You* are going to drink your wine and relax while I figure out what needs to happen so I don't have to watch you cry again." He leaned over to grab my glass, and I squeaked, tightening my arms around his neck, though the single hand on my ass held me to him just fine.

"You think I'm going to drop you?" With a raised brow, he stood upright like he hadn't been seconds away from letting me land flat on my face and strode to the back window that opened up to the roof.

It wasn't exactly a deck and definitely wasn't up to code, considering there was no railing, which was probably why he loved going out there so much. It was his space. Whenever I'd come by on Wednesday nights and let myself into the apartment, he would be just climbing in from outside. This, though, was the first time he'd ever invited me out there with him.

"Well, you almost did," I said.

"I'd never let you fall." And the way he said the words, the soft timbre of his voice against the shell of my ear, sounded like he was talking about an awful lot more than just dropping me.

CHAPTER FIFTEEN

BECK

FOR AS LONG AS I'd lived here, this had been my sacred space. The one place I could go and not have to contend with anyone else. I didn't even invite Ford out here, and he was closer to me than anyone.

But I couldn't deny that it felt natural to have Everly here beside me.

Most people wouldn't be impressed with it. There were no chairs, no tables, no strings of those fancy lights everyone lost their shit over. Usually, I didn't bother bringing anything out at all, just sat right on the hard roof with nothing but my thoughts to keep me company. But for Everly, I'd grabbed an armful of pillows and blankets and had tossed them into the corner, making it as comfortable as possible for her.

With how the structure was built, we had our own little alcove tucked away from prying eyes. It faced the ocean, with two sides open and the other two comprised of the building, which meant the corner was the perfect nook for us. The closest cottage was fifty yards away, so we might as well have been totally and completely alone, just how I preferred it.

Everly sat bracketed between my bent legs, hers outstretched in front of her and crossed at the ankles. I rested her wineglass on my knee as she reclined against my chest, and I just breathed her in, a unique blend of her usual scent mixed with mine that made my cock twitch.

She hadn't said much since we came out here, but thank Christ she was no longer crying. In the entirety of our friendship, I'd never seen her cry like that—had never seen her shed more than a couple tears while watching a movie or a commercial that tugged at her heartstrings. Not even when she'd first moved here and was overwhelmed with the transition of the business and being in a new place. She'd taken it all in stride—almost irritatingly so.

I was the downer of our duo. She was an eternal optimist, someone who didn't let life get her down. So when she'd started crying—no, *sobbing*...huge, gut-wrenching sobs that had torn at my heart—I knew she'd been pushed to the point of no return. And I fucking hated that it'd happened when I was supposed to be taking care of her. Though I didn't exactly see a way around this—I couldn't go back in time and stop the fire, couldn't save any of the contents of her home or magically create a new clinic for her, so I had to support her however I could.

But the issues weighing on her definitely put into perspective what I'd been worried about earlier today. In the end, it didn't matter if I was apprehensive or scared or nervous about what was going on between us. Everly needed me, plain and simple, and I had no intention of disappointing her.

"On a scale of one to breakdown, where are we now?" I asked against the shell of her ear.

She vibrated against me with a laugh and twisted around to look up at me, the move shifting her ass against where I was already rocking a semi for her. The faint light from inside my apartment cast a shadow across her face as she grinned up at me. "Maybe like a four?"

I made a gruff sound in the back of my throat and splayed my hand over her stomach, holding her tightly to me. "Still too high."

"Well, just because you said things weren't weird between us so they're magically not, that doesn't mean you can say my house and business didn't burn down and have it be true. They're both still charred, I still have to replace everything, and I still have to figure out how I'm going to see patients."

"I told you not to worry about it."

"Beck." She sighed. "I have to worry about it, because if I don't, it's not going to get done."

Except that I already told her I'd take care of it.

"You can renew your license online, so no DMV hassle. You have an appointment tomorrow at the bank, and I sweet-talked Charlotte into compiling a list of numbers for credit card companies so it'll make calling for replacements easier."

Everly was quiet for long moments, and I had a brief panic that I'd overstepped. Then she said, "*You* sweet-talked someone?"

I exhaled a heavy sigh, relaxing my tight muscles. "Fine, I bribed her."

Everly's laugh was loud and carefree and the best thing I'd heard all fucking day. "What in the world did you bribe her with?"

"She wants my blueberry scone recipe, but I had her settle for a portable charcuterie spread for her to bring to the beach for fireworks on Friday."

"Well, I don't blame her. Your spreads are delicious." She reached over and plucked one of the last crackers from the tray I'd brought out for her. "And that was very devious of you."

"I'll be as devious as I need to be to get you taken care of."

She breathed in deeply and exhaled, relaxing into me as she linked her fingers over mine on her stomach and squeezed. "You're too good to me."

She'd still cried today, so I was definitely going with not good enough.

"It seems you weren't just cooking Chuckanut dinner while I was gone," she said. "You've been kind of busy, huh?"

I shrugged, bringing her the glass of wine for a sip and accepting it again when she was done.

"Well, I guess that only leaves the most important and most daunting part," she said. "How am I still going to see patients?"

"That's probably the easiest."

"How in the world is that the easiest?"

"House calls."

"House calls?"

"I'm sure that's a foreign concept to you big-city dwellers—"

She laughed. "Bellingham is hardly a big city."

"—but we're very familiar with them here. I think your aunt did them back when she remodeled the clinic."

"That's a really great idea..."

"Then why do you sound hesitant?"

"Well, it *is* a good idea, but I don't have any way to actually *do* house calls. My car got damaged, too, remember?"

Yeah, I remembered. I recalled every word the chief mentioned of the damage done to Everly's place while she'd stood there, eyes glazed as she'd leaned into me like she hadn't been able to hold herself up.

"What kind of alternate reality are we in that *I'm* suddenly the one finding a way to make things work and you're throwing up roadblocks? Just take my truck. There. That's settled. Anything else weighing down that gorgeous mind of yours?"

She breathed out a sigh and relaxed back into me. "Only one last thing…"

I ran through the list of issues in my head, unable to come up with anything I hadn't already covered.

"I just need to figure out where I'm staying."

With me, that was where. I didn't want her anywhere but here. Didn't want her figuring this out on her own—especially when she was already overwhelmed. That would lead to stress, which would lead to exhaustion, which would lead to her skipping meals because she was too busy or just plain old forgot, which was a downward spiral she'd gone down too many times to count. And I refused to let her do it again.

"You're staying with me."

"But eventually—"

"You're staying with me," I said, firmer this time.

"I feel like we've already had this discussion."

"We have. A couple times. So can this be the last?"

"You promise you're not going to get sick of me? What happens when you reach your limit of Everlyness?"

I was starting to believe my limit for Everly did not exist.

"Don't worry about it because it's not going to happen."

"Easier said than done."

"Sounds like you're thinking too much." I reached for the wine bottle and topped off her glass before handing it to her. "No place else to be tonight, so you can get as drunk as you want and forget about all this other shit."

With her head resting against my chest, she tipped it back and stared up at me. "How come tonight is get Everly drunk, but you don't even have a beer?" She furrowed her brow. "Actually, I don't think I've ever seen you drunk... Why is that?"

Well, fuck. I hadn't been prepared to talk about this tonight. Or ever. And I could still keep it to myself...could feed her a bullshit story and not have to sift through the mountains of baggage piled on my shoulders. But Everly had cracked herself open in front of me today. She trusted me with her tears, so I could trust her with a tiny piece of my history.

I took a deep breath and exhaled slowly. "Because I saw what too-much looked like before I even knew what alcohol was, and I decided a long time ago that was never going to be me."

She was quiet for long moments before she finally said, "Your dad?"

"Yeah."

"Do you want to tell me about it?"

I swallowed, having no idea how to share this with someone because I'd never had to. The only people who were remotely close enough to me to warrant knowing about it had already lived through it, same as I did. But I found myself...*wanting* her to know. Wanting to share this part of myself with her that I hadn't shared with anyone else.

"He lost his job when I was maybe thirteen? That was the

beginning of the end. He was a functioning alcoholic for most of my childhood. He wasn't a mean drunk. Didn't hit us or anything. He was just...absent. Too worried about his own shit to worry about us. Which meant everything fell on my mom's shoulders—the house, the resort, us kids. All because my dad could never be without a glass of gin." I huffed out a breath and shook my head. "I still can't stand the smell of that shit. His whole life was consumed by it, and our lives revolved around whether or not he was drinking. Our days started super early just so we could fit in what we needed to before he was drunk. But every year that went by, his start time got a little earlier and earlier, until pretty soon, he was drunk by noon."

While he'd never been physically abusive, he'd still neglected me. *Us.* Whether it was outright ignoring us as he tucked himself away, forever working on *the next great American novel* rather than job hunting or helping Mom with the resort, or just straight passed out in the living room at four in the afternoon.

"I'm sorry, Beck."

"Yeah, well. It is what it is. I just decided I didn't want to do that. I've been drunk exactly once."

"Really? When?"

I cleared my throat. "The day they found my mom's boat but not my mom."

My dad had been drunk then, too. Passed out on the couch while my brothers and I had stepped in, taken the reins, and figured out what to do, all the while looking after Addison and worrying that the only guiding force we had in our life was gone.

I'd spent a lot of years wishing it'd been him who'd been on that boat and not her, wondering why the hell a good person and an amazing mom was taken too soon when someone like my dad continued dragging his ass through life, barely existing.

Everly made a soft sound in the back of her throat and pressed a kiss under my jaw. "That's a lot for you to deal with. I can see why you made that choice. What about the rest of your siblings?"

I shrugged. "It affected us all differently. I think I'm the only one who doesn't really drink. I'll have a beer here or there, but that's about it." I held her wineglass in front of her. "But it doesn't bother me if anyone else does, so drink up."

"Would you hold my hair back for me if I spent the night puking?"

What the hell kind of question was that? "You know I would."

"Well, it doesn't matter because it's not happening."

"Why not?"

She didn't answer me right away, and it was too dark to be able to read any nuances in her expression.

"Sunshine?"

She took a deep breath, the move pressing her even more tightly against me. On an exhale, she said, "Because if I'm drunk, you won't let us have a replay of this morning."

I froze behind her, all thoughts of my parents and my rocky childhood vanishing into thin air, replaced by the memories of her in the shower, her back to me, ass tilted up as I slid my cock between those lush thighs, her moans in my ears as I came against her.

"What makes you think I will anyway?" I asked, but my voice was too deep, too ragged to pass for casual.

She shifted against me, very deliberately rubbing her ass against the erection I couldn't hope to hide from her. "Just took a wild guess."

Fuck. What was the right thing to do here? She wasn't drunk—she wasn't even tipsy. She'd probably had a total of one glass, and since she'd stuffed herself on the tray of meats, cheeses, crackers, and blackberry vanilla bourbon jam I'd brought out for her, she was good.

And my willpower was crumbling.

I tucked my face into her neck, pressing my nose against her skin and inhaling deeply. She smelled so fucking good, and she was so soft and warm against me, and she was wearing my shirt even though she had half a dozen others to choose from, courtesy of Luna. And now, her tight little ass was right up against my cock, taunting me, tormenting me, and I wasn't sure I could resist any longer.

She reached over, plucked the glass from my hand, and set it off to the side. Then she leaned back against me, slipping her hands on top of mine and threading our fingers together as she brought them to her stomach. "Stop fighting it."

With her guiding the way, she slipped our hands beneath the T-shirt, my fingertips grazing over the soft skin of her stomach, up her rib cage, and not stopping until our hands were cupping her bare tits.

"*Fuck.*" I couldn't stop from clenching my hands, groaning when her nipples pebbled against my palms. "What do you need, sunshine?"

"You," she breathed, arching into my touch and pressing her ass more firmly against me.

And that was it. All bets off. Game over. I was done for, blissfully annihilated at the hands of this gorgeous siren.

CHAPTER SIXTEEN

BECK

WITH EVERLY'S whispered admission playing on a loop in my mind, I was totally and completely lost to her.

"Stand up," I said, probably sharper than I should have, but she complied immediately, and I didn't waste any time, yanking her leggings down and groaning when her naked ass came into view. "*Sunshine*. You've been walking around with a bare pussy all day? Sitting in my lap with only a flimsy piece of cotton keeping me from your sweet cunt?"

"Yes," she breathed, looking back at me over her shoulder, and I couldn't wait another second. Couldn't wait for her taste on my tongue or her moans in my ears.

I spun her around and cupped her ass, pulling her to me as I affixed my mouth to her. There was no lead-in, no buildup. I swiped my tongue through her slit, groaning at her sweetness, and sucked her clit straight into my mouth.

She cried out, and I fucking loved that I could evoke those reactions from her. I wanted to soak up every single one, revel in the fact that *I* was doing this to her. But it was too loud, considering we were outside. And though no one could *see* us up here, there was no fucking way I wanted anyone but me hearing what Everly sounded like when she came. If I needed to cover her mouth and capture those sounds in my palm so they were just for me, so be it.

With one final nip to her clit, I turned her back around, biting her perfect ass before tugging her into my lap. I hooked her legs outside of mine, and then I spread them, opening her up completely as a breeze gusted through. She shuddered against me, a soft whimper leaving her.

"That feel good, sunshine? You like having your pussy exposed like this?"

She moaned her response as I ran my hands up the outside of her legs, over her knees, and down her inner thighs, stopping just shy of her pussy. And then I retraced my path all over again.

Into her ear, I said, "I've thought about this all fucking day. I've wanted you again from the second I came against you in the shower. Wanted to slide inside that gorgeous cunt and fuck you right there."

"Yes," she breathed, dropping her head back on my shoulder as she gripped my thighs, shifting her hips as she chased my touch. "I wanted that too."

Despite her words, I continued my path, torturing us both and never letting myself touch her pussy, skating along everywhere but where we both wanted it. "Are you wet for me, sunshine?"

"*Yes.*" She rocked against me, seeking my fingers and the pleasure I could give her.

Christ, I wanted to feel it—how hot she was, how wet and tight. How *needy* she was for me. I wanted to make her come hard and fast, but the buildup was half the fun, and after the day she'd had, she could use a little of that.

"Show me how you want me to touch you," I said against her ear.

"What?"

"Take my hand and show me how you play with your pussy. Use me to get yourself off."

I wanted to know every way to get her there, every touch she craved, every stroke that made her wild. Wanted to learn every single one of them and use them on her over and over again. Everly always did what others wanted her to, what they expected of her. If I accomplished nothing else during our time together, I was going to teach her how to be greedy with me. I wanted her to know she could always, *always* be selfish with me, and I'd sell my soul to the devil to give her exactly what she needed.

She whimpered at my words but did as I asked, placing her right hand on top of mine and threading our fingers together before slowly dragging them down her inner thigh, toward her pussy. Instead of going straight for her clit like I expected, she brushed our fingers everywhere but, stroking them along the crease of her leg, along her pussy lips, featherlight touches that would've driven me fucking insane. But not Everly. She panted in my lap, her breaths coming hard and fast. She rested her head against my shoulder, her face turned toward me, eyes closed as she used me to touch herself, and I'd never seen anything more gorgeous in my life.

My cock was a steel bar in my jeans, hard and throbbing and desperate to feel her wrapped around it. I wanted nothing more than to slide into that heaven and lose myself in her.

Finally, she split our fingers into a V and pressed them down on either side of her slit. She was drenched and so fucking ready to be filled, but still, she kept on teasing. Up and down, up and down, incrementally closing the distance between my spread fingers with each pass until finally there was constant friction on either side of her clit. She rocked her hips against me, the rhythm matching our every stroke, the touch making my already hard cock throb. And then on the next downstroke, she slipped my fingers inside her, and I nearly came in my fucking pants. She was hot and tight and wet and so goddamn perfect, I wanted to sink all the way inside her and never leave.

I groaned against the shell of her ear. "I fucking knew it. I knew that greedy little cunt would be dripping for me."

She shuddered against me, her breaths growing quicker while she worked herself with my hand. Over and over, she rocked against my fingers, guiding me how she wanted it. How she needed it. On the next downstroke, just as I slipped my fingers inside her, I shifted, widening my legs and opening hers even farther, spreading her completely.

"*Beck.*"

I clamped my left hand over her mouth, trapping her moans against my palm. Against her ear, I said, "Shh, baby. Those sounds are just for me. Fuck, I wish I could see you like this. Writhing in my lap, that pretty pink pussy spread open and ready for my cock. Shove your shirt up. Let me see those perfect tits."

She scrambled to do as I asked, one hand still on top of mine as we played with her pussy while she lifted her shirt up with the other. Her chest was heaving, nipples tight and begging for my tongue, and my mouth actually watered at the thought of sucking them deep, of tasting every inch of her skin.

"Good girl." I scraped my teeth along her earlobe, my cock throbbing at her answering whimper. "I want them in my mouth, but that's not gonna happen right now. Not when your pussy is pulsing around my fingers like you're about to come. You close, sunshine?"

She hummed against my hand, her hips shifting restlessly as we worked her pussy together.

"Can you do something for me?" At her nod, I said, "I need you to play with your tits. Pinch those gorgeous nipples. Not soft, though. Hard. You like a little pain, don't you, baby?"

With a moan, she released my hand between her legs

and cupped her tits, pinching her nipples just like I asked her to. She was a writhing mess on my lap, her pussy so wet, she was dripping down onto my jeans, and I fucking loved it. Loved that I'd gotten her here—that *we'd* gotten her here together—made her so desperate for it she was soaked.

I slipped my middle and ring fingers all the way inside her, pumping them quickly while I ground my palm against her clit. Jesus fucking Christ, she was perfect. I could hear how wet she was, how needy she was for me, and the thought alone nearly had me exploding like I was fifteen all over again.

"I fucking love how greedy you are for me. Your pussy just sucks me right in, doesn't it? Can't wait to see you spread tight around my cock. Can't wait to feel you come all over me."

Her entire body went taut as I pumped my fingers into her faster, harder, curling them inside her, and then she exploded. She moaned into my hand, the sound trapped against my palm as her pussy tightened around my fingers, her hips rocking with every pulse.

I groaned into her neck, relishing the feel of her coming apart at my hand, at my touch. "That's my girl. Such a good fucking girl. God, you're so gorgeous when you come for me, aren't you? So goddamn perfect."

I was hard as granite, my cock throbbing in time with her pussy clenching around me, and I wanted nothing more than to finally slide inside her and fill her completely. Wanted to catch her moans on my tongue while she writhed on my cock, aching for more.

But not now. She'd had a hell of a long day, and I wasn't going to push, no matter how desperate I was to feel her around me. So instead, I dropped my hand from her mouth, resting it at the base of her throat, my thumb grazing her skin. I slowed my pumping fingers, lightening my palm against her clit until it was just a whisper of a touch where she was still so fucking wet for me.

"Beck..." she whispered, shifting her hips, seeking the pressure and friction I wasn't giving her.

I hummed into her neck, pressing a kiss against her heated skin. "Good?"

"So good." She wrapped her hand around my wrist and squeezed. "But I want more."

Her words froze me in place, my cock aching and desperate for relief, already leaking for her. But apparently I was a masochist who couldn't accept when a good thing —a *perfect* thing—writhed in his lap.

"Not tonight."

She made a frustrated sound in the back of her throat and tightened her grip on my wrist, pushing my fingers deeper inside her, causing us both to groan.

"Quit trying to say no to this," she said, her voice thick with desire. "You always know what I need and give it to me, even when I don't ask. Well, right now, I'm asking. I need this. I need *you*."

I froze for a heartbeat...two, three... And then I

snapped, unable to hold back any longer when I'd been doing so for years. I sat forward with a growl, forcing her down to her hands and knees in front of me. She squeaked but bit her lip, glancing at me over her shoulder as I fumbled with the fly of my jeans before shoving them down. She didn't wait, either, tugging her shirt off and exposing everything to me, just as impatient for this to happen as I was. Then she looked back at me with lust-hooded eyes, and I was completely fucking gone for her.

I gripped the base of my dick and squeezed, hoping with everything I had that I wasn't going to slide inside her and lose it in one thrust. "You need my cock?"

"Yes," she breathed.

"You want me inside you?"

"God, Beck, *yes*."

That made two of us. I wanted it more than anything. Had wanted it for years, and I was fucking tired of suppressing it. Tired of ignoring the urge that never went away when I was around her. I'd never wanted anyone as much as I wanted her, never ached for someone like I did for her. She was my sunshine, and I was caught in her orbit. There was never any possibility this would end any other way.

But this was *Everly*. I was supposed to fuck her slow and sweet. Soft, just like she was. Except I couldn't even wait to get her inside my apartment—I had no fucking idea why I'd thought gentle would ever be a possibility with her. Not when I'd waited years for this. Not when she was arching her back and glancing at me over her shoulder, lips parted and eyes heavy with lust, everything about her begging for me. For my touch and my lips and my cock.

And I had no intention of depriving either of us a second longer.

I slid my dick through her slit, groaning at how wet she was as I rubbed the head back and forth over her clit, making her gasp. "You need to be quiet, sunshine, or I'll have to cover your mouth again."

She bit her lip and nodded, shifting her hips to try to work my cock inside her, and I was tired of making us wait. I'd wanted this woman for years, and tonight, I was having her.

I gripped her ass, digging my fingers into her lush curves as I notched myself at her entrance. And then I gritted my teeth, stifling my groan, as I slowly sank inside. Despite how wet she was, she was so fucking tight, I had to work myself in, inch by painfully slow inch. Everly whimpered with each pass, her body gradually welcoming me until, with one final thrust, I seated myself completely into the sweetest, tightest heaven I'd ever known. Her body fit mine like a glove, her pussy stretching around me and welcoming me in like she was made for me. Like we were made for each other.

"*Beck.*" She collapsed down on her elbows, bracing her forehead on her hands, the move tilting her hips and allowing me to sink even deeper. "Oh my God."

"Jesus, Everly. Oh *fuck*." I pulled back before sliding in again, and a sharp gasp fell from her lips.

Gravel crunched on the path, and the soft cadence of voices reached us. People might not be able to see us, tucked back here on the roof, but there was no doubt they'd be able to hear us.

Reaching forward, I wrapped my fist around Everly's hair and tugged her back toward me until I could whisper against her ear. "You've gotta be quiet, baby. There are people down there, and I don't want anyone to know how good I work this pussy. How much you love my cock inside you. No one but me."

She nodded quickly, her eyes wild as I tugged her hair harder, making her arch her back toward me. God, she felt too good. Too tight and wet and warm, and there was no way I was going to last. Not after two years of my right hand being my only companion. Not when her sweet pussy was my homecoming.

"Rub that needy little clit for me." I cupped her tit, tugging on her nipple as I scraped my teeth against the side of her neck and sank them into the juncture at her shoulder. "You're gonna be a good girl and come all over my cock, aren't you?"

With a whimper, she reached down, sliding her fingers through her slit, all the way down until they were on either side of my pumping cock.

"Jesus Christ." I gritted my teeth as she tormented us both, running her fingers through her slit, down to my cock, and then playing with my balls like I wasn't already three seconds away from blowing inside her.

I let go of her hair and wrapped my hand around her throat, tugging her until her back was flush against my chest. With my other hand, I reached down and slapped her clit hard enough to pull a gasp from her as she jerked against me. Her pussy contracted around my cock, tugging me even closer to the edge.

"If you need to scream how good it feels, you better turn your head." I pumped into her faster, strumming her clit, my knees nearly buckling at how tight her pussy was squeezing me. "Give me all those fuck-me sounds right against my neck, baby."

She whimpered and turned her head toward me, her panting breaths washing over my skin and making my cock even harder. My balls drew up tight, and I had to clench my ass to keep from losing it before she came.

"No more playing, sunshine," I gritted out through clenched teeth. "I'm so fucking close. I need you to come. Soak my cock and show me who owns this pussy." I tightened my hand around her throat, holding her against me as I pinched her clit just hard enough to give her the whisper of pain she needed, and she went off like a rocket.

She pressed her mouth against my neck just like I told her to, her moans vibrating against my skin as she pulsed around me, and that was all I needed to fall. With a groan, I sank deep and came, barely holding in the animalistic groan I was desperate to unleash knowing there was nothing between us as I spilled myself inside her.

Holy fucking hell, that was the best sex of my life, and I hadn't even gotten undressed. I'd taken her out here on the roof on her hands and knees like a goddamn animal. I hadn't given her flowers or candles. No music but the rhythmic sound of the waves lapping at the shore.

But I had no idea why I ever thought it'd be any different with her. Not when she drove me so fucking wild with want and crazy out of my mind with need that I couldn't see straight. Couldn't see anyone but my sunshine.

Next time, though. Next time, I was spreading her out on a bed and feasting on her pussy until she couldn't move. Until she was begging for me to stop. And then, when she was so swollen and wet from my tongue, I'd finally sink inside and make her come all over again.

And I couldn't deny it anymore—there would absolutely be a next time. Because there was no way I could walk away now.

CHAPTER SEVENTEEN

EVERLY

MAYBE ONE DAY I'd be tired of waking up with Beck's mouth on my pussy, but today was not that day. The past three days hadn't been it either.

After the night on the roof, it'd been like the dam had broken and unleashed all the pent-up want and desire we had for each other. He was insatiable. *I* was insatiable, which was totally new for me. Though apparently that happened when you were super comfortable around your partner and said partner actually knew what they were doing and was more concerned with your pleasure than their own. We hadn't been able to keep our hands off each other. I felt like I'd swapped places with one of the heroines in my books, and I was absolutely here for it.

I groaned, reaching down to thread my fingers through Beck's hair as he sucked my clit into his mouth. I glanced down, finding his eyes already on me. And sweet Jesus, the sight of this man with his mouth between my legs would never fail to send my stomach flip-flopping like I was on a roller coaster, speeding down a hundred-foot drop.

I'd spent years worrying about anything and everything during sex, rarely able to reach orgasm, and then Beck had barreled his way in and wouldn't allow me to do anything *but* focus on him when we were together. Whether it was his actions or his words, he had my attention completely.

He slipped his fingers inside me, pumping them in time with the rhythm of his tongue against my clit. He felt so good against me, already knowing just what I needed to make me come. I was climbing, climbing, climbing—almost there, but never falling over the edge, and I nearly groaned at the buildup, desperate for relief.

Beck pulled back, still thrusting his fingers into me, and sank his teeth into my inner thigh just hard enough to sting, his eyes heating at my moan. "Give it to me, baby. I'm starving. Come all over my tongue so I can lick up all that sweetness."

I whimpered, desperate to give him what we both wanted, and he dove back in, sucking my clit while he pumped his fingers deep inside me. It all felt amazing, but it wasn't until he reached up with his other hand and tugged my nipple hard enough to make me bow off the bed that I exploded. I clutched his face against me as waves of ecstasy pulsed through my body, the soft slide of his tongue and the slow pump of his fingers bringing me down from my peak. When the last wave rushed through me, I blew out a contented sigh and relaxed back on the bed, spent and sated.

And then he started all over again.

I twitched, my body still oversensitive, but Beck didn't care. Loved it, in fact, and had told me as much when he'd wrung more pleasure from my body than I thought possible. He'd done this enough times that I knew what he was after—namely, another orgasm courtesy of his exceptionally talented tongue.

But I wanted more. I tightened my hold on his hair and tugged until he finally relented and braced himself above me, his eyes glittering as he sucked me off his fingers.

"I wasn't done," he said, the rasp of his early morning voice sending a shiver skating down my spine. "My plan was to make you come three times with my tongue."

"Well, my plan is to get you inside me." I hooked a leg around his waist and tugged him closer, biting my lip when his cock nudged my clit. "And since I was the one whose house burned down, I get to make the rules."

"*Sunshine,*" he said, the admonishment clear in his tone as he glared down at me.

I bit my lip to stifle my laugh, but it managed to slip out anyway. "Are we not at the joking stage yet?"

"It's been three days since I held you while you soaked my shirt with your tears. No, I'm not at the fucking joking stage."

"My bad," I said through a giggle, and his scowl only deepened.

I wasn't necessarily at the joking stage, either, but what else was I supposed to do? I'd gotten what I could handled —my replacement credit cards and license were on the way, all non-emergency appointments had been shuffled around and rescheduled for house calls this coming week and surgeries had been referred to the next closest clinic about an hour away, and the insurance adjuster had already been out to survey the damage.

While, yes, my home and business had been demolished and I didn't have a possession to my name, I was now pretty much living with my best friend, having the best sex of my life, and figuring things out.

Sure, my stomach was churning basically nonstop because my parents still asked me about moving home during every phone call—which had been daily since the fire—and my brother was still on my shit list, thanks to him souring Beck for my parents, and I was still overwhelmed at the thought of what to do with regard to the clinic, not to mention my home. But I wasn't focusing on any of that. I couldn't. If I did, I'd have another breakdown like I had the night Beck had taken me out on the roof, and I did not want to go back to that place again.

So instead, I shoved all of that down and focused on the here and now. On Beck's gorgeous, muscled body spread out on top of mine, his hips resting in the cradle of my thighs, his cock so hard and thick between us that I ached to feel him inside me again.

I'd *never* enjoyed sex before. Well, that wasn't entirely true. It was fine. Perfunctory. A task to check off my to-do list. But I'd never felt anything close to what I read about in my favorite books. I'd assumed it was all hyperbole.

It was *not*.

Though it shouldn't have been a surprise that sex with Beck was incredible. Not when everything else with him was so perfect. He already knew how to play my body, though I had no idea why I thought it'd be any different. He'd been reading romances with me for months—had borrowed my print copies and seen every highlighted or flagged passage, every dog-eared page. Had a front-row seat to every kink, every encounter, every dirty word that piqued my interest.

And he'd exploited them.

Not that I was complaining. Not when he was the Everly Whisperer and had been able to figure out things about me even I hadn't. I had more than a decade of experience making myself come, and I still hadn't realized I liked a little pain with my pleasure. Somehow, Beck had been able to suss that out after our first time together. He spent his time studying me as he wrung every ounce of pleasure from my body, which would explain all the multiple orgasms.

Well, that, and the fact that he was really good with his fingers. And his mouth. And his cock.

My *God*, his cock.

"Are you too mad at me to fuck me?" I asked.

He sat back on his heels, hooking my legs over his own and spreading them as he ran the head of his cock through my slit. "I'll never be too anything to fuck you."

"Does that mean you'll give it to me whenever I want?"

"Just say the word, and I'll slide inside this sweet pussy anytime you want."

"*Word.*"

The corner of his mouth ticked up, and he notched his cock at my entrance, slipping the barest inch inside. Every thrust stretched me a bit more, my pussy greedy for him to fill me like only he could. He teased us both with shallow thrusts and brought my left leg up, resting my foot on his shoulder. Running his hand up and down my calf, he split his focus between my face and where he was disappearing inside me, pushing in a little more with each thrust but never giving me what I wanted. What I needed.

Groaning, I reached down, digging my fingernails into his thighs. "*Beck.*"

"Sunshine." Keeping his eyes locked with mine, he turned his head and brushed his lips along my ankle while he caressed my calf, light, barely there touches. So soft and gentle, and not at all what I needed right now. I wanted him filling me up, stretching me to the brink until he was all I could feel, all I could think about, all I could—

He thrust deep, sinking his teeth into my skin and pulling a moan straight from my soul. "Fuck," he said on an exhale, staring down at where he sank all the way inside me, my pussy stretched tight around him. "How can you feel so goddamn good every time?"

I shook my head, knowing exactly what he meant but too lost in the sensations he evoked in me to speak any of that aloud. All I could manage were gasps and moans as he filled me up over and over again, his cock stretching me with every thrust.

He cupped my ankle with one hand and splayed the other on my lower stomach, his fingers spread as he circled my clit with his thumb. "Look at you," he said, his voice a low rumble against my skin. One I felt all the way to my bones. "That pretty pussy's wrapped so tight around my cock, taking me all the way in."

I moaned at his words, at the soft touch of his fingers on me, tracing around where I was stretched open around him. Light, scarce touches that did absolutely nothing but drive me out of my mind.

"Beck, I need..." I exhaled a sharp breath, lost in the feel of him.

"What?" he asked, his fingers a whisper against me, his thrusts slow and deep. "Tell me what you need, and I'll give it to you."

"More," I breathed, curling my fingers into his thighs.

"Show me." He flipped us then, rolling us until he was beneath me and I sank down fully onto his cock.

"God," I choked out, barely able to make even that single word. Bracing my hands against his chest, I tipped my head back and groaned as he filled me completely, our bodies meshing in a way I'd never experienced before. I closed my eyes and circled my hips, gasping when my clit brushed against him, sending a zing of pleasure through my body.

"Fuck yeah. That's it, sunshine. Rub that pretty little clit against me. Use my cock however you need, baby."

I rested against his bent knees and rocked back and forth over him, unable to look away from his face. His hair was mussed—from sleep and my fingers—lips parted and eyes heavy-lidded as he split his attention between my face and where I took him all the way inside me.

"Jesus," he rasped, eyes heated as he brushed a thumb over my clit. "You're taking me so good, baby. So fucking good."

He was so deep this way, it was hard to know where I ended and he began. And as much as I loved this slow rock...staring down at him as he looked up at me with awe and something I couldn't quite name in his eyes, it wasn't enough. I needed him in charge, needed him guiding me, *fucking* me.

"More," I breathed again, trying and failing to get the kind of speed, the kind of friction I needed. "Please, Beck. I need more."

He reached up, cupping me on the back of the neck and tugging me forward until our lips met. He took my mouth with his own, sliding his tongue along mine as he brushed his hands down my waist, over my hips, until he cupped my ass in his palms.

Against my lips, he said, "Hold on, baby."

I barely had time to register what he meant before he snapped his hips up, thrusting his cock so deep inside me, it stole my breath. He held me above him and drove into me from below, fast and hard and a little rough... Exactly how I needed it.

"God, yes," I breathed into his mouth, my fingers curling into his chest.

Still holding me, he reached from beneath and traced around where I was taking him deep, gathering my wetness along his fingertips. Then he cupped my ass again, his fingers just ghosting near my back entrance, and I snapped my eyes open, locking them with his.

A full-body shudder ran through me at the slightest glance of his fingertips. Holy *shit*, I'd never felt anything back there at all—had thought for sure I wouldn't like it, but there was no denying the way my pussy fluttered, my clit throbbing with just the lightest of brushes...the barest hint of his touch.

Beck groaned. "Fuck, I can feel you. You're close, aren't you, baby? Pinch your clit for me, sunshine. I want you to choke my cock and gush all over me."

With a whimper, I snaked my hand down between us, my chest pressed to his as he held me above him and thrust into me over and over again. All the while, he brushed his fingers back and forth, never quite passing over my back entrance, but close enough that it brought forth a rush of sensations, my pussy thrumming in time with his thrusts.

Beck's chest hair rasped against my nipples, and all it took was a barely there brush of my fingers against my clit before I detonated, my body bursting into a thousand tiny pieces as I came apart.

"Fuck yes, baby, that's it. That's my good girl. Such a perfect little pussy coming all over me. *Christ.*" With two more thrusts, he groaned and settled deep, his warmth spilling into me as he shuddered through his release.

I collapsed against him, both of us breathing hard as my pussy pulsed around him through my aftershocks.

Moments later, when I'd finally caught my breath enough to speak, I said, "Holy shit."

He pressed his lips against my forehead, his fingers still clutching my ass, softer now but no less claiming. "I was going to say holy fuck, but yours works too."

I breathed out a laugh and turned my head, propping my chin on the back of my hand. "So...that was new."

Beck just raised a brow—he'd barely touched me, after all, hadn't so much as slipped the tip of his pinkie finger inside my ass, but it'd definitely been enough to send me spinning and pique my curiosity. "Good new or bad new?"

"Let's just say that now I know why maybe there's no talking before the characters dive right into butt stuff."

His eyes heated as he stared up at me, clenching his fingers on my ass, his cock jerking inside me. "Noted."

"Well, don't note it too hard. I'm thinking, like, a note card, or maybe even a Post-it. I don't want the whole legal pad," I said, squeezing my pussy around his way-too-large-to-go-anywhere-near-my-ass cock.

He laughed, a full-bellied rumble, and I couldn't help but smile in return. I adored this side of him—I adored *all* sides of him, but I'd never seen him so happy. So carefree. And I liked to think maybe I had a little something to do with it.

Chuckanut barked from her bed in the living room—her kennel had always been her safe space, so I was so relieved she'd transitioned easily into her new one—demanding attention, namely in the form of breakfast.

Beck rolled us to the side before kissing me. "I'll take care of her. You go jump in the shower."

He stood and stepped into a pair of gray joggers, and I bit my lip as his perfect, sculpted ass disappeared beneath the cotton. He was really too hot to be legal, like one of my book boyfriends come to life.

Striding out, he left the door open enough for me to hear his conversation with my dog. "Morning, Chuck. Your mom's in there ogling me and being too much of a pervert to take care of you, but I've got it."

I pressed my head back into the pillow and laughed, wondering how the hell I'd gotten so lucky with him. And how it'd taken me two damn years to see what was right in front of me all along.

CHAPTER EIGHTEEN

EVERLY

AFTER MY SHOWER, I strolled out to the scent of bacon. Beck stood in front of the stove, wearing nothing but that pair of gray joggers slung low on his hips and his backward baseball hat, and Christ on a cracker, he looked good. Like, *super* good. Like, he should be on a calendar for hotties who can cook. It really was as if he'd stepped out of the pages of one of my books—a book boyfriend come to life. The perfect man.

Okay, not perfect. He was grumpy and got a little grouchy when I used his apparently very expensive fancy jam for toast and forgot to hang my damp towel up after a shower—whoops, I needed to remember to do that. But he loved my dog and treated her like a human, kept his cupboards stocked with my favorite foods, brought me chocolate and pain relievers when I was on my period, and watched full seasons of a show he hated because *I* enjoyed it and it made me happy. He fed me amazing food, was the best cuddle partner I'd ever had—even before nakedness had come into play—and he could make me forget about everything else when I was with him. Not to mention that he made me come like a freight train.

So he might not have been perfect, but he was pretty perfect for me.

Not wanting to announce my presence just yet, I stayed just out of view so I could have unfettered access to watch him and Chuckanut. She sat dutifully at his bare feet, head cocked and focus on him as she waited patiently for any and all scraps to land her way.

"I don't know why your mom insists on feeding you garbage." He glanced down at her, his voice low. Probably because he most definitely wouldn't want me hearing this. "But I'm working on it. You like what I feed you better than that other shit, anyway, don't you? If you agree, just sit there and stare at me."

He raised a brow at Chuckanut, who, predictably, sat there, staring up at him. I pressed a hand over my mouth to stifle a giggle, but apparently I didn't do a very good job, because he snapped his gaze in my direction. A scowl settled on his face when he found me peering around the corner.

I walked toward him, shooting him a grin. "Uh-oh. Have I overstayed my welcome already?"

"No," he said, the crease in his brow deepening as he turned back to the stove. "But you don't get any bacon."

"Well, that's not very nice."

"It's also not very nice to spy on people."

"I wasn't aware you were sharing state secrets with my dog." I leaned my hip on the counter next to him and raised a brow. "Do we need to invest in some sound-proofing for the closet so you can have your clandestine conversations in there?"

He stared at me, mouth pressed in a flat line, before jerking his head toward the table. "Go sit."

With a laugh, I pushed off the counter and started toward the table. I made it only half a step before he snagged me around the waist and tugged me back to him, not stopping until our bodies were pressed together, my hands braced on his bare chest.

"Wait." He danced his fingers along the hem of my new sundress that hit mid-thigh, dropping his face to nudge the thin strap at my shoulder with his nose. With his lips against my skin, he said, "I like this."

But he somehow made those three innocuous words sound dirty. Hell, *everything* sounded dirty coming from his mouth, especially after three days of nearly nonstop sex. And if we weren't fucking, he was giving me his sex eyes or whispering all the filthy, depraved things he wanted to do with me while we were supposed to be watching a movie or walking Chuckanut or cooking dinner.

He cupped my chin, tilting my face up toward his. Then he brushed a thumb over my bottom lip just before he captured my mouth with his. Sliding his fingers into my hair, he kissed me slow and deep—so different from the usual way he devoured me, but I was absolutely not complaining. I melted into him, opening my mouth as he slid his tongue against mine, the soft groan that poured out of him sending shock waves straight to my clit. My nipples tightened beneath the fabric of my dress, and my body ached for him already, despite that he'd been inside me not even an hour ago.

Finally, after we were both breathless and I was nearly a puddle of goo against him, Beck pulled back. "Now you can sit." Then he smacked my ass before turning back to the stove like he hadn't completely wiped my brain of all thought.

I wanted to shoot a pithy retort back at him, but the truth of it was, it took all I had just to make my way to the table without tripping over my feet like a newborn colt. God, the things this man made me feel.

Would it always be like this with him? This urgency, this need he'd awakened that had only managed to grow in the time we'd been together was unprecedented for me. Was it just because it was new? That magical time in all relationships when everything felt unbelievable? Or was it because it was Beck? Because he'd been my best friend and closest confidant and my rock, first and foremost, and my...whatever he was second?

Beck placed a heaping plate of food and a glass of orange juice in front of me, effectively pulling me out of my thoughts. Then he plated a dish for Chuckanut—the berry egg oatmeal he'd perfected for her—before dishing up himself.

When he sat down perpendicular to me, I raised my brow, then pointedly looked down at my plate where, despite his warning, bacon was piled high on the dish next to a frittata with heirloom tomatoes, spinach, goat cheese, and asparagus. "No bacon, huh? What do you call that?"

He didn't even glance my way, completely focused on his own breakfast. "The burned pieces. Worse than no bacon at all, if you ask me. I won't even feed it to Chuck."

I pressed my lips together and nodded. The strips weren't burned—they were cooked to perfection, crisp and juicy, just how I liked them, and I moaned when the salty goodness melted on my tongue.

Beck's gaze darted to mine, his eyes heating as I devoured the totally not-burned deliciousness.

I squinted an eye and pointed a finger at him as I chewed. "Don't even think about it."

"What?"

"Don't give me that look. Your sex eyes aren't going to work on me."

"Sex eyes?"

"Oh, don't pretend like you don't know what you do." I lifted my foot and poked his thigh, but before I could lower it back to the floor, he grabbed it, settling his hand on my ankle and keeping it right in his lap. "We should actually leave the apartment today and do something more than walk on the beach."

"Then quit moaning at the food I made you like you do when my cock's in your mouth."

I huffed out a breath, my pussy tingling at the imagery that evoked. Just last night, I'd slipped from the chair and knelt before him, tugging his cock out of his pants as I showed my appreciation for him turning on another episode of *Gossip Girl*. I'd intended for it to be all about him, but he'd only lasted a couple minutes in my mouth before he'd had me bent over the chair as he fucked me.

"Beck," I said, though the admonishment fell flat, considering the breathy tone of my voice.

He shrugged a single shoulder and ran his thumb up the arch of my foot as he took another bite of his breakfast. "It's the truth."

"Maybe so, but we can't stay in bed all day."

"Says who?"

"Your friends down at the farmers market."

Every Saturday, Ford opened the diner so Beck could hit the local market and purchase the food he'd need for the diner that week. It was something I'd never been able to attend since the clinic was usually open Saturdays until noon, so I was excited to join him.

"Thought my grumbly face scared away all my friends?"

"Not everyone finds it as endearing as I do, that's true." I took another bite of the delicious breakfast, holding in another moan. "But you need fresh ingredients, and Chuckanut needs to walk off the pound of organic bacon you fed her."

"It hasn't been a pound."

"It's been enough."

"Well, *someone* has to make up for the years of shitty food she's been eating her whole life. And I don't want to point any fingers as to who's been giving her that garbage, but it was someone in this room, and it wasn't me and she doesn't have opposable thumbs, so..." He squeezed my foot, the warmth of his hand a comforting weight against my skin.

"Yes, yes, your all-organic feasts are delicious, and you're treating us both like queens. Now, can we go to this thing? I promise we'll be back home before too long."

Beck's eyes flashed with an emotion, but it was there and gone before I could pinpoint it. "Fine. But you better be wearing something over that tiny-ass dress unless you want me fucking you behind a food cart."

Images of that flashed in my mind, and I bit my lip. Ever since we'd read *Forbidden Temptations* last month, exhibitionism had been on my radar. The thought of Beck taking me where anyone could see us sent a shiver down my spine.

He leaned forward so his lips brushed my ear, his voice only a low rumble as he said, "Who's the dirty one now, baby?"

CHAPTER NINETEEN

EVERLY

I WASN'T sure there was a cuter town in the world than Starlight Cove. It was so picturesque—when I'd first moved here, I'd asked the mayor if the Hallmark Channel had ever used the downtown area because it looked like it was straight out of a movie.

All along Main Street, flowers overflowed from the large baskets that hung from each of the black streetlamps. This section of town was closed off by blockades on Saturday mornings to stop traffic from interfering with the market. Though they probably wouldn't have needed any since nearly all of Starlight Cove attended this every week.

The street was packed with people browsing, several walking their dogs, which meant if Chuckanut wasn't trying to make friends, I was. Each time I squatted down to introduce myself to a new dog or reacquaint myself with one I already knew, I'd smile up at Beck to find him staring down at me, his lips quirked at the side.

Finally, knowing we were on a time crunch, I stood, guiding Chuckanut through the market. "Okay, no more doggie time or we're never going to get through all of this. It's so much bigger than I thought it was going to be!"

Beck glanced over at me, a brow raised.

I rolled my eyes and swatted his stomach. "Don't be a pervert."

"I don't know how you expect me to be anything else when you basically said that same thing the first time you saw my dick."

"Well, it was intimidating. You try being my size and facing a one-eyed Pringles can monster."

Beck inhaled sharply, which threw him into a coughing fit. Good. It served him right.

I patted him on the back, not even trying to tamp back my grin. "You okay?"

"Fine," he croaked with a nod.

I hooked my arm back through his as we strolled, holding Chuckanut's leash with my other hand. "Seriously, though, I thought it would just be a couple booths with some produce. I didn't think it would be all of this."

There had to be fifty tents stretched along either side of Main Street, containing all manner of goods, from fresh fruits and vegetables to homemade taffy and jam to candles and lotions and various other products. It was a cornucopia of Starlight Cove's offerings.

"It didn't use to be this big," Beck said.

"No? What was it like?"

"When my mom first started it, it was just a handful of people."

"Your mom started this?" I asked, soaking up any bit of information I could about his family or his past. Even after two years of being friends with him, I was still uncovering parts of him. But that was Beck for you, and I had a feeling I would still be peeling away layers in another two years.

I didn't mind, though. I loved each time he revealed a little bit more of himself because it was confirmation of our bond deepening.

"Yeah, that was my mom in a nutshell," he said. "When she saw a need, she filled it. She needed ingredients for the diner, and the people around Starlight Cove needed a way to sell their excess food. This was one of the things I helped her with."

That was very apparent, as we couldn't go more than five feet without someone calling out for Beck or waving as we passed by. He never stopped to chat—that absolutely wasn't him—but no one seemed to mind. They still offered him a smile and a wave as we made our way through the market.

Usually, he was the quiet, introspective one out of the pair of us, but this time, I watched, loving that I was able to witness him in his element. He went from stand to stand, scrutinizing every ingredient as if he were a judge on a cooking show, his eyes hard and assessing.

After the fifth stop without him buying anything, I finally said, "So are we just window-shopping, or...?"

The side of his mouth kicked up, and he glanced down at me. "I want to see everything that's available first. Then I'll plan the menu and buy what I need."

I froze, pulling us to a stop in the middle of the street. "Wait a minute. You plan it here?"

"Yes."

"*Now*?"

"Yes?" he said, though it came out like a question.

"Whoa. I thought...well, I assumed you had it already planned before you came and were just, like, grocery shopping."

"Can't plan the menu until I know whether the tomatoes or asparagus or berries are going to be shit this week or if they've got a good crop."

"Right. Nobody likes shitberries. They taste nothing like their cousin, strawberries."

He glanced over at me, the barest hint of a smile tugging on his lips, and shrugged. Like it was no big deal. When in reality, it was blowing my mind.

"You're out here, making full menus to feed who knows how many people, and I can barely make a box of mac and cheese."

"That would explain why you never have any goddamn food in your house."

I laughed and started us along the path again, guiding

Chuckanut ahead of us. "Why would I when my best friend—now boyfriend—is an amazing chef?"

Beck's eyes flared hot as he glanced over at me, and it took me a minute to figure out what I'd said. When I did, I bit my lip, wondering if I'd overstepped. If I'd read the situation wrong. Were we just friends with benefits? We hadn't had that discussion yet, but it felt like a whole lot more than that to me.

Finally, he asked, "Is that what I am?"

I swallowed down my apprehension and uneasiness and played it off. "An amazing chef? Obviously." Before he could say anything else, I squeezed his arm. "You're kind of amazing all around, you know that?"

If I hadn't been looking at him, I would have missed the tips of his ears turning the barest shade of pink.

My grin widened, all my previous uneasiness gone. "I can't believe all the dirty, filthy things you've said to me, and *this* is what embarrasses you?"

"If you don't watch yourself, I'm going to take you behind one of those stands, hike up that flirty little skirt, and say more of those things while I fuck you." He shot me a heated gaze, all traces of his embarrassment gone. "Don't think I didn't notice Chapter Fifteen in *Forbidden Temptations* flagged."

This time, I was the one blushing, no doubt looking like I was walking around with two lipstick smears on my cheeks with how hot my face felt.

"Beck, there you are! Come here for a second, will

you?" Mabel waved from her booth, effectively cooling the tension between Beck and me. Her husband, George, sat beside her, hands folded over his round belly and his head tipped back as loud snores poured from his open mouth.

"Mabel has a booth?" I whispered. "What does she—"

"If you value your sanity, you won't ask."

She didn't have anything on display—just a large banner with a graphic of a finger in front of a pair of red lips, like they were shushing everyone. What kind of secret society nonsense was this?

When we made it to her, he just raised a brow. "Yes, Mabel?"

"Well, I was thinking about that deal we made, and I was wondering if—"

"No."

She huffed. "But you don't even know what I'm going to ask!"

"Still no. A deal's a deal."

"Wait, what deal?" I asked.

"Nothing," Beck said at the same time Mabel blew a raspberry and said, "Before he'd give me back my phone, he demanded that I never speak to you again."

Beck scrubbed a hand over his face. "Jesus Christ, Mabel. I told you not to ask her specifically about the fire. That's it. You're not even recording right now. Why do you feel the need to embellish absolutely everything?"

She sniffed, tipping her face up, her nose in the air. "It's the journalist in me."

"You're not a journalist. You're a busybody."

"I'll have you know, I—"

Beck and Mabel continued squabbling, but I couldn't find any words, my heart too full over what he'd done for me. I hadn't asked him to, hadn't said a word about not wanting to share that pain with anyone but him, but still, he'd known. Though, I shouldn't be surprised. Beck had shown time and again that if something would make me happy and he had the power to take care of it, there was nothing he wouldn't do for me. Even more amazing was that I rarely even had to ask.

"Are we done here?" Beck asked, though he did so in a way that didn't leave much room for argument.

Mabel huffed. "Fine. We're done."

"Great, let's go."

"Wait!" I said, tightening my arm through his before he could walk away. "What do you sell?"

Beck exhaled a deep sigh and pinched the bridge of his nose. "Why'd you do that?"

Mabel completely ignored Beck as her face brightened. She reached under a tablecloth and pulled out two huge baskets overflowing with bottles of what looked like—

"Lube!" she said, loud enough that the vendors across the street probably heard. "The fuddy-duddies on the town council don't think it's 'appropriate' for me to have these on display because it's a 'family-friendly' event. How the hell do they think we got all these families in the first place? That's what I want to know." She set the

223

baskets on the table with a flourish. "Anyway, we compromised. I'm still allowed to rent a booth, but I can't show the products unless someone comes up and asks. And if you're interested in the toys, you have to book a party."

"The toys?"

"Oh yes! You know, lots of men are intimidated by a woman using adult toys to reach her pleasure, but they should really be looking at them as more of a partner. Some of my top sellers can be used on the clitoris during pene—"

"Oh, look," Beck said loudly, talking over Mabel, "there's Brady and Luna." And then he tugged us away without a backward glance.

"Just call me whenever, sugar, and we can set something up!" she called after us.

"Holy shit." I breathed out a laugh and stared up at Beck, eyes wide and mouth agape. "Mabel sells *sex toys*," I hissed.

"Yeah. I told you not to ask. Now, I'm going to have nightmares for a week."

"Well, maybe I should book a party since all my toys are ruined. Or are you one of those men who are intimidated by a little help?"

Beck's eyes flared as he stared down at me. "You and I both know you don't need any help when I'm around, but if you want to, I'm all for recreating Chapter Eight from *A Night for Her Pleasure*. But unless you want our sex life to be broadcast on a Facebook Live, we're not buying them from Mabel."

"Noted," I breathed, thoughts of recreating Chapter Eight with Beck floating through my mind, and my clit tingled in response.

"Get that look off your face," he said. "I don't want to talk to my brother while I'm hard enough to pound nails."

With a laugh, I bit my lip and nodded, trying my hardest to focus on any and everything but Beck using a toy on me, but it was damn difficult.

Fortunately, Chuckanut had no such issue with distraction and led us straight to Luna's booth. I shouldn't have been surprised that the sheriff of Starlight Cove had secured his girlfriend a prime spot, but there they were, right in the middle of where traffic was the heaviest.

I'd never seen two more mismatched people in my life, but somehow it worked on them. Brady stood off to the side, his large, muscled arms crossed over his chest, looking like a pissed-off bodyguard, while his girlfriend, Luna, flitted around. She wore an off-the-shoulder shirt, a flowy skirt that went down to her ankles, and a bright smile so heavily contrasted against Brady's scowl it was nearly comical. She waved at people walking by even as she helped a customer, all while Brady glared at them like he was paid to do so.

A man in his early fifties was attempting to bargain with Luna, and Brady's attention was solely on the two of them, so we patiently waited our turn.

Beck leaned over, his lips against my ear. "Watch...it's about to get good."

Before I could ask him what I should be watching for, Brady leaned forward, plucked the glass jar of homemade face cream out of the man's hands, and set it right back down on the table with a loud thunk. "Get out of here."

The man sputtered, eyes wide. "Excuse me?"

"You heard me." Brady jerked his head to the side, dismissing the man with as little effort as possible. "Get lost."

Luna breathed out a laugh and rolled her eyes. "The grump's coming off a little strong there, Sheriff."

With his eyes still locked on the man, Brady said, "If he doesn't want to pay what they're worth, then he doesn't deserve them at all."

I didn't recognize the no-longer-potential customer, and it was clear he was a tourist because he obviously didn't recognize Brady. Ninety percent of the town's population would've been running before Brady could even finish his sentence.

Finally, this guy seemed to get a clue and realize Brady was, indeed, being serious, and he stalked off, grumbling under his breath about rude giants. If I wasn't mistaken, Brady's lips actually twitched at that.

Luna rubbed her fingers on her temples. "Babe. Seriously. You can't keep doing that."

He just stared down at her, brow raised, massive arms crossed over his chest—honestly, did he lift houses for fun? "Did you or did you not work with Aiden to calculate the cost you should sell these for?"

"I did."

"And did you or did you not mark your products at those prices?"

She sighed. "I did."

"Then they're going to pay what the goddamn price sheet says, or they're not getting them at all."

"Um...should we come back?" I asked, not wanting to interrupt but feeling a little uncomfortable during their spat.

Brady and Luna, who stood toe to toe in some kind of a standoff, both answered without turning in our direction. "No."

"They're like this all the time," Beck said, grabbing one of the taffies Luna had out in a dish.

Without taking his eyes off Luna, Brady reached out, plucked the candy from Beck's hand, and put it right back in the dish.

"Seriously?" She huffed out a laugh. "You're not even allowing your brother a piece of candy now?"

"Is he buying anything?"

"Brady." Luna reached out and gripped his forearm. "I'm going to stop inviting you to help me at these if all you're going to do is scare off the customers."

"I hate to tell you this, but he's not exactly the kind of guy who cares about getting an invitation," Beck said. "He'll just show up."

"He's not wrong." Brady shrugged.

Luna laughed and dropped her head back on a groan. "I love you, but you are driving me crazy. Why do you keep doing this?"

"Because you work too hard on this to have some schmuck wearing socks with his flip-flops to try to swindle a deal. You turn our house into a fucking science lab, use me as your guinea pig, and pour your heart into every goddamn one of those jars." Brady pointed to the plethora of various creams in all different sizes of containers on display. "You're fucking amazing, and you know what you're doing because my hair has never been so soft, so you're going to get paid what you're worth. And we're not discussing it anymore."

Luna kept a straight face for several long moments, and I held my breath as I watched this unfold. Finally, she rested her hands on his chest, stared up at him, and said, "Okay."

"No, I told you. You're not— Wait. Okay?"

"Yes. Okay." She nodded. "You're right."

"I *am* right."

"Thank you for reminding me what I'm worth."

With a hand cupping her ass, he hauled her into him, lifting her right off her feet as he kissed her deep. My eyes went wide as I watched because, yeah, things were definitely heating up, considering this was a supposedly family-friendly event. If Mabel couldn't have lube on display, I was thinking foreplay was probably also discouraged.

Beck cleared his throat loudly. "All right. I'd appreciate it if I didn't have to watch my brother make out anymore. Jesus Christ."

Luna laughed and pulled away, tapping Brady on the shoulder until he put her back on her feet. "Hey, guys. Sorry about all that. I'm happy to see you out here, Everly."

"Thanks, I'm glad I could come. The clinic's usually open on Saturday mornings, so I haven't had a chance to yet."

Luna's eyes softened. "How are you doing? Getting settled okay?"

"Yeah. I'm staying with Beck. There have been a couple of close calls, but he hasn't kicked us to the curb yet."

Beck tightened his hold on me, a move that didn't go unnoticed by Brady if the twitch of his eyebrow was any indication.

Luna laughed. "The McKenzie boys' barks are worse than their bites—all of them. Well, except for Ford. I don't know if that guy has an ounce of bark in him."

"Then you haven't seen him around Quinn yet," Beck said.

Luna's brows lifted. "Noted." To me, she said, "Hey, if you ever want to get away or need some rejuvenation time, swing by the main inn. Yoga class or a massage on me."

It was an amazing offer, and one I normally would've

jumped at. Luna was seriously a magician with her hands, and her yoga classes were some of the best ones I'd ever taken. But what stopped me in my tracks wasn't the offer but the fact that I didn't feel like I needed it. Except for the night the chief had been by to see me, things were going...fairly well. I still didn't know what was going to happen or what I was going to do, but I wasn't focusing on that. Right now, I was focusing on the present. On being with Beck and enjoying this life all my own that I'd carved out in Starlight Cove.

CHAPTER TWENTY

BECK

ON MONDAY, my family—minus that lucky shit, Levi—gathered in the diner for a meeting. I told Addison and Aiden that the only way I was showing up was if it was here, so they finally relented. I wasn't an early riser under normal circumstances, but especially not now. Not when I spent hours worshipping Everly's body each night and then again before she could slip out for her run in the mornings.

She'd been living with me, for all intents and purposes, for nearly a week, and things were going far better than I expected. Though that didn't take much since most of my thoughts circled around fire and brimstone. It was in my nature to wait for the other shoe to drop, but I was finally putting that out of my mind when it came to her. To us. Besides, considering how we got together, I figured all the shoes had already dropped.

"Okay, so just a quick update," Addison said. "Bookings are still steadily coming in, and we're full into August now. We also have our first wedding scheduled, and I'm thinking about contacting Harper and pitching an article to her. Maybe Dream Weddings on the Coast or something like that."

"You clear that with Levi?" I asked.

Addison rolled her eyes. "I'm not going to clear it with Levi. If he wants a say in this kind of thing, he needs to get his ass to these meetings. Otherwise, he's just going to have to pull up his big-boy pants and deal with whatever history he and Harper have together like a grown-ass man. Good?" Addison waited half a second before continuing. "Good. Aiden and I have been handling the increased volume, but we may want to look into hiring some staff—at least for cleaning. Probably only part time to start."

My brows lifted. "Like...someone outside the family?"

"Yes."

"Who we'll pay?" Ford clarified.

"Yes," Addison answered, her loss of patience obvious in her tone.

"With...actual money?" I asked.

"Oh my God, *yes*," she snapped.

"Uh..." Ford glanced around at all of us. "Are *we* going to start getting paid with actual money?"

"You do get paid with actual money," she said.

"Oh, sorry, when I asked that, I thought it was clear I

meant enough money so we could do more than buy a pack of gum once every two weeks."

"Your weekly stipend is on top of room and board and enough food to feed an elephant," Aiden said, his tone all business. "And don't think I haven't noticed the extra amount on this week's food order, Beck. Just because Everly's staying with you doesn't mean we're footing the bill for her, too."

"He has a point," Addison said. "It wasn't a big deal when it was just coffee, but now we're paying for her meals, too? If we don't want the resort to slide back into the red, we really need to watch these kinds of things."

Ford glanced my way, and I knew we were thinking the same thing—sure, they didn't notice that I'd been dropping off a shit-ton of food each week for the past ten years to Cottage Thirteen, but *this* they noticed.

Before I could tell them to fuck off, Aiden dove into the numbers—more for Addison's benefit than anyone else's—effectively making my eyes glaze over until the bells on the door jingled.

Everly slipped inside, a grin on her face as Aiden continued boring everyone to death. "Hey," she said, a little breathless from her run.

Her hair was pulled back in a ponytail, her cheeks flushed, and I wanted nothing more than to remove the tiny scraps of fabric she called running clothes, bend her over the counter, and feast on her for breakfast.

Instead, I handed her the coffee I'd already prepared

and studied her face, looking for any tells that she was nervous or apprehensive about her first day of house calls.

When I didn't find any outward signs of unease, I asked, "You good?"

The grin she shot me could've powered a rocket for all it did to my heart. She needed to figure out how to bottle that shit and sell it. "I'm good. First appointment is in an hour, though, so I better run. I'll swing by around noon to let Chuckanut out."

"I've got her. Don't worry about it."

"You sure?"

"Yep. Your lunch is in the fridge."

"You made me lunch? What is it? No, wait. Don't tell me. I want it to be a surprise." Her eyes brightened, a smile lighting up her face. "I'll call you later and let you know how it's going."

"Good." Without thinking, I leaned in and kissed her, our lips barely touching before we both froze.

She pulled back, staring at me with wide eyes that very clearly said, *Did you seriously just do that?*

And, yep, I seriously did just do that. In front of my entire fucking family. A pin dropping could have been heard, considering the silence that descended on the diner. She breathed out a laugh and shook her head, then turned, leaving me to deal with the fallout all by myself.

"I'll see you tonight. Bye, everyone." With a wave, she pushed through the front door and strode outside, past the wall of windows and toward the stairs that led to my apartment.

And even when the bells on the door stopped jingling, silence still reigned.

Avoiding the elephant in the room, I pulled out my wallet, plucked two dollars from inside, and held them up. "Here. Happy?" Then I stuffed them in the register to more than cover Everly's coffee.

Unfortunately, that didn't get so much as a peep. No one said anything for a solid minute, but I sure as hell wasn't going to be the one to break the silence. Not when the nosy bastards would want to know everything about my relationship with Everly, and the truth was, I...didn't know. I didn't know what this was between us. She'd slipped and called me her boyfriend at the farmers market, but that was as far as it'd gone. Was that what I was? I could admit now I wanted to be a whole lot more than that, but the label didn't matter to me as long as she was *mine*.

Finally, Aiden cleared his throat. "Like I was saying, profits are up, and if bookings remain steady, then—"

Addison slapped her hand down on the table, loud enough to make Ford jerk upright from where he'd been resting his head on his folded arms.

"What the fuck, Addison?" he grumbled. "Don't make me pay attention to this. You know I'm not a numbers guy."

"How am I the only one freaking out about this?" she asked, her tone about five octaves higher than usual.

"About what?" he asked.

"About *what*? Are you serious?" She stared at each of us, mouth agape. "Oh, I don't know. How about the fact that Everly just strolled in here to get her morning coffee, and Beck kissed her like it was no big deal?"

Ford shrugged. "I already knew."

"You already *knew*?" she spat, each word an accusation.

"Same here," Brady said.

Addison whipped her head in his direction. "*What*?"

He stepped behind the counter and refilled his coffee, completely unconcerned that our baby sister was losing her shit. In Addisonland, that was just another Monday. "Was I supposed to put out a bulletin or something?"

She pressed her fingers to her temples. "Okay, I get the secrecy from Ford because 'twin bond' or whatever," she said with a roll of her eyes, "but *you*? Why the hell didn't you tell me?"

He stared at her over the rim of his coffee cup, brows raised. "Guess it'll forever remain a mystery."

Addison huffed before turning to Aiden and pointing a finger at him. "What about you?"

He shrugged. "Didn't know."

"And you don't *care*?"

"Not particularly. I mean, great. Good for them." He lifted his chin in my direction, the equivalent of a five-minute cuddle in Aiden's world, and I accepted it with a nod.

She opened and closed her mouth as she split her gaze

between the four of us, exasperation written on every inch of her face.

"Is there a reason you're freaking out about Beck and Everly becoming Beverly?" Ford asked.

"Don't ever say that again." I shook my head, crossing my arms over my chest, and leaned against the counter.

"What? I thought it was catchy. Better than Evereck. That's just stupid."

"Are we about done here?" Brady asked, but he didn't wait for a reply before he put a lid on his to-go cup and headed for the door.

"Yep," Aiden said, gathering up his things before following closely behind Brady.

"I'm out, too," Ford said. "And before you ask, Sergeant, yes, I'm working on the list." With a salute, he strolled out the front door, bells jingling in his wake.

And then it was just the two of us. At least until a couple walked in and sat in the back booth. I greeted them, took their orders, made their breakfasts, and still, Addison hadn't said a word. She *never* kept quiet, as proven in great detail following the kiss. Something was up, and I was too intrigued to let it go.

Finally, after I'd dropped the check off at the couple's table, I braced my hands on the counter and stared her down. "Seriously. What gives?"

"Nothing!" she answered too quickly, her gaze focused on her tablet, her fingers flying like she was *oh*-so busy.

"Addison."

"So Chuckanut is upstairs?"

"Yeah? I figured you'd lose your shit if I let her in here."

"You can't have a dog in a restaurant."

I raised my brows as if to say, *See?*

"You think that's a good idea?" she asked. "Getting her acclimated to your apartment when she's probably not even staying there for long?"

My stomach clenched at the thought of Everly anywhere but there. Anywhere but my bed. It was way too early in this relationship to discuss living arrangements with her—we hadn't even confirmed the boyfriend/girlfriend thing—but if I had it my way, her name would already be on the lease.

Even so, Addison wasn't one to concern herself with the emotional stability of a dog.

"What's this really about?" I asked.

"I'm worried about Chuck!"

"Addison. You're not worried about Everly's dog. And I'm really fucking confused as to why you'd suddenly have a problem with Everly and me together when you've been hinting at us hooking up for over a year. Now that we finally do, you're suddenly freaking out about it? What gives?"

She finally lifted her gaze from her tablet and glanced my way. "Fine. I just...I'm worried, okay?"

"About?"

She braced her elbows on the counter and leaned closer, dropping her voice. "Look, I'm happy for you. This is the first time you've put yourself out there with, well, anyone but your own freaking twin."

"And that's not a good thing?"

"Not when the person you're putting yourself out there for has one foot out the door."

I froze, my entire body going cold at her words. "What does that mean?"

"It might be nothing, okay? You know what? It probably is. Just forget I even said anything and—"

"Addison."

She blew out a heavy sigh as she slumped her shoulders. "You remember the day after the fire, when I took Everly shopping?"

"Yeah."

"Well, she called her parents while I ran into the last store. I got back in the car while they were still talking."

That wasn't new. Everly's parents were the kind of parents movies were made about—married for forty years, still happily involved in their children's lives. Hell, I wouldn't be surprised if her mom knit them matching holiday sweaters. Everly usually talked to them on Sundays, but there hadn't been a day that'd gone by since the fire when they hadn't called to check in.

"They were really pushing for her to move home," she said, her voice quiet.

"And?"

"And... Well, she didn't outright tell them she wasn't."

The vise around my chest squeezed tighter. "Well, did she tell them she *was*?"

Addison shook her head. "Not exactly. She said she wasn't moving home *now*. Not that she wasn't moving home ever."

I breathed out a heavy sigh, relief flooding me. At least until I thought about some of the clipped conversations I'd heard between Everly and her parents. She was stressed whenever she hung up, but I'd assumed it was because her parents were worried about her and she was picking up on it. But maybe it was because they were pushing for her to move home, and she didn't know how to tell me.

"Maybe it's nothing," Addison said. "I just don't want you to get in too deep if she's only going to leave in the end."

Well, that was the problem, wasn't it? I was already in too deep. Had been for a long fucking time. I'd been in love with Everly longer than I wanted to admit, and that sure as hell wasn't going to go away now. Not when I knew what she tasted like, not when I'd held her in my arms as we slept. Not when I'd been inside her.

I just had no idea if she felt the same. No idea if what was left for her in Starlight Cove was enough to keep her here.

242

CHAPTER TWENTY-ONE

EVERLY

FOR MY FIRST day of house calls, I most definitely should've brought more than one change of clothes, considering the number of times I'd been peed on.

Normally, having an extra outfit at the clinic was more than plenty, but I'd forgotten I was seeing two different litters of puppies today. And though being on the bottom of a puppy pile first thing on a Monday morning was great for my spirits, having said puppies use me as a urinal was not.

It wasn't even noon, and I was already exhausted. This was turning out to be a hell of a lot harder than I'd been anticipating. I was expecting smooth appointments since all the animals would be relaxed because of the environment. And though they were definitely more comfortable in their own homes, that also meant they roamed everywhere and didn't stay where they needed to for an exam. I didn't mind chasing them around or rolling on the floor to get them interested enough in me so I could do what I needed to, but that just added on to each appointment time.

And those appointments just kept butting up against each other, which amped up my anxiety, which the animals definitely picked up on.

April and I also hadn't scheduled enough transit time between each appointment, which was causing a complete clusterfuck since I was already running behind. And, okay, that was probably due in large part to the fact that I was driving—and I used that term loosely—Beck's truck. Which also happened to be a stick. Which I also happened to have pretty much zero experience driving.

Okay, I had none. No experience driving a stick shift—except for one very unfortunate instance in high school—but I'd figured it out because my car's engine had been damaged in the fire, and I didn't have another choice.

With the number of looks I'd gotten as I attempted—poorly, mind you—to change gears while driving down Main Street, I wouldn't be surprised if Beck had received a dozen calls about it by now.

Jerking to a stop at the small, pale-blue house for my next appointment, I cringed at the sharp grinding coming from the transmission and prayed I hadn't destroyed his vehicle. If my living with Beck hadn't challenged our relationship enough, this certainly would.

I grabbed my bag—a poor substitute for a clinic full of

equipment, but I made do—and climbed out, hustling up the front lawn even though I was already fifteen minutes late. This was a routine well-check appointment for Esther's cat, who was usually so relaxed even at the clinic she was damn near comatose. Hopefully that meant this would be a quick in and out, and I'd be able to make up some time and get back on track with my schedule.

I stepped up to the front door and rang the bell, gripping the handle of my bag in both hands while I waited for Esther. After several moments when there was no movement that I could hear coming from the other side of the door, I tried knocking, a bit louder than I normally would in case she was at the back of the house.

When there was no answer, I walked around the side door and tried that instead, just in case.

Still nothing.

I pulled out my phone and checked the time. Another five minutes had already gone by. I now had only ten to complete the appointment, and even then, I'd only just be back on time.

There was no fence, so I walked farther back, poking my head into the yard to see if maybe Esther was taking a quick break. Nope. Since there was a window on the door to the garage, I peeked inside. Empty.

Well, that was just fantastic.

With a sigh, I leaned back against the door and called April. It rang once before going to voice mail.

If you're calling for me personally, hang up and send a text like a normal person. If you're a patient and are calling for Dr. Bowman, please note that my lunch is from noon to one, and I do not answer calls during that time, even while I'm working from home.

"Dammit," I said under my breath and ended the call.

It was now twenty minutes into her hour-long lunch break—something I'd kill for right about now. Or even just five minutes to scarf down some food. The meal Beck had made and packed for me was languishing away on his kitchen counter because I'd forgotten it in my rush to leave. And I was using a new purse since my last one was destroyed, which meant I didn't have any long-lost stash of snacks stuck in a pocket somewhere.

My phone rang, a picture of Beck and me at Movies in the Park lighting up the screen. I was leaning back against his chest while I cheesed for the camera, and he was looking down at me, the barest hint of a smile on his lips. It wasn't perfect, but I loved it. I swiped to answer as I headed back to Beck's truck, frustrated and hungry and still smelling faintly of pee, and now I was missing a patient. "Hello?"

There was a pause, then, "What's wrong?"

Tears pricked the backs of my eyes for no good reason. "How do you know something's wrong?"

"Sunshine."

With a heavy sigh, I opened the door to his truck and climbed in. "It's just...today's not going how I thought it would. Everything's screwed up and taking longer than usual, and now Esther stood me up for my appointment after we squeezed her in today because she said it was imperative."

"And you're hungry."

I breathed out a laugh. "You found my beautiful lunch on the counter?"

"Yep. Come by, and I'll make you something."

"God, I wish. I don't have time, though."

"Where are you?"

"In front of Esther's house, being stood up like a chump."

"You're at her house? Why are you there?"

"Um...because we had an appointment?"

"But it's Monday."

"I mean, I get that Mondays are awful, but that doesn't give her an excuse for standing me up."

"No, I mean, she runs bingo at the senior center on Mondays. Brings Jingles there, too."

"What? Why the hell would she schedule an appointment for when she wasn't even going to be home?"

"I'm guessing she figured you'd know where to find her."

Well, I probably should have since I'd lived here for two years. And if this was as routine as Beck said, that was over one hundred instances that I'd never noticed. God, I still felt like a newbie around here. Hell, Luna seemed to be acclimated more than I was, and she'd only been here a couple months.

"Okay," I said, though my voice wasn't very strong. I cleared my throat and tried again. "I'll head there. Thanks."

"Hey, are you—"

"I've gotta run, but I'll see you tonight, okay?"

Beck paused, then finally said, "Yeah, okay. But call me if you need anything. And eat something."

"I will." I hung up, gripping the steering wheel and blowing out a heavy sigh—no time for food or pity parties, so I forced down my frustration and ignored my rumbling stomach. Then I started the truck, shoved it into gear, and headed in the direction of the senior center.

I didn't make it half a block before my phone rang again, and I couldn't glance over to check caller ID, so I answered without checking, assuming it'd be Beck again.

"I'm fine. I promise."

"Not how I thought you'd answer the phone," Ash said. "But it's good to know you're not still mad at me."

I blew out a heavy sigh. With how my day had been going, I definitely should've expected this. "I *am* still mad at you."

"Why? I went to Jamaica like you told me to."

"You *ran* to Jamaica, and you did it after tattling to Mom and Dad about what an awful human being Beck is and leaving me to deal with the fallout. The same Beck, by the way, who's given me a place to stay after my house burned down."

"Oh, I bet he's giving you a place to stay, all right."

"*Sebastian.*"

The line went quiet, then he said, "Um...holy shit. Okay, so you're *actually* mad at me, then. Look, I'm sorry, okay? I just—Jesus, what the hell is that noise?"

"I'm driving a stick," I grumbled.

"Like...you're dressed up as a witch and it's your pretend broom? Because I know you don't mean a car. Don't you remember what happened when you were a junior and you—"

"*Yes.* I remember. Look, now's not a great time, okay?"

"Yeah, I'm getting that. What's going on?"

There was no way in hell I was going to tell him everything that was swirling through my mind because he'd only fan the flames.

Instead, I said, "It's just been a long week."

"It's Monday."

"The most Mondayest of Mondays ever."

He was quiet for a minute, then said, "Hey, remember the house you love? The little yellow one on Maple Street with the porch swing and the cherry tree out front?"

"Yeah?"

"Well, it just went up for sale."

"Okay..." I said, drawing out the word. I didn't have time to talk about this.

"What do you mean 'okay'? I thought you'd be losing your shit about it."

"Why would I do that?"

"Uh, maybe because you've been lusting after it for

years? You have a secret board on Pinterest filled with decorating ideas for it, for fuck's sake."

"What's your point?"

Ash blew out a heavy sigh. "Look, you and I both know Starlight Cove isn't right for you. Just come home, Evie. Mom and Dad are salivating for it—Mom's already planning the first week of meals she's making when you come back. And I miss you."

"Well, that's too bad because I hate you."

"No, you don't," he said, nothing but affection in his tone. "You love me. And you miss me, whether you want to admit it or not."

The truth was, I did miss the little asshole. And after the day I'd had, home sounded damn good right now.

Beck

IT WAS after seven by the time I walked into the apartment, Chuck greeting me at the door. She wove in and out of my legs, her tail wagging fast enough I was surprised she didn't achieve lift-off. I squatted down to give her some love and accepted the puppy kisses, while my focus was elsewhere.

Everly sat in my chair with *Gossip Girl* playing on the TV, and a bowl of Starbursts sat on the side table next to a glass of wine. Before I even got a good look at her, I knew what I was dealing with.

Her shit day had only gotten shittier.

That was confirmed when she spun the chair around and looked up at me. Her face was clear of makeup, her hair piled in a knot on top of her head. She wore one of my T-shirts and nothing else as far as I could tell. And she looked exhausted.

Chuck jumped up in her lap with the kind of exuberance only a dog could muster, even though she'd probably just been sitting with Everly before I came home.

"Hey," she said to me as she ran her hand softly down Chuck's body.

And, yeah, this wasn't going to do.

I snapped my fingers and pointed to Chuck's luxury bed in the corner—yeah, it was a little over the top, with its platform feet and tufted cushions, but her house burned down, too, and I wanted her to feel comfortable in my place, so I'd bought it for her. The dog leaped down, trotting over and jumping up to her throne, then she proceeded to walk in four full circles before curling into a ball with a sigh.

Squatting in front of Everly, I rested my hands on the outsides of her bare thighs, thumbs brushing along her soft skin. "Hey." I studied her eyes, which were usually so bright and full of life. But not now. Now, though they were clear of tears—thank fuck because I wasn't sure I could handle another crying situation so soon—there was no denying they weren't as vibrant as they usually were. "What's wrong?"

She lifted a single shoulder. "I'm... It was just a really long day."

"Yeah? You want to tell me about it while I eat your pussy?"

That startled a laugh out of her. "Beck."

"What?"

"I'm pretty sure going down on me isn't the answer to every problem."

"But I'm pretty sure it could be the answer to *this* one. You think you'll be able to remember what was so bad when my tongue's inside you?"

She closed her eyes and breathed out a laugh, shaking her head. "Oh my God."

I pressed a kiss to her knee. "Tell me how your day went from amazing this morning when I kissed you goodbye to bad enough that you're watching *Gossip Girl* and mainlining Starbursts and wine."

She blew out a heavy sigh, her shoulders slumping. "The house calls were a complete disaster."

"It was your first day. I'm sure it'll take some time to iron out the kinks."

"I hope so, because who knows how long I'm going to be doing this."

"It won't be forever. Just until you can get the clinic rebuilt."

She huffed out a laugh. "Well, that's the thing. I got a

call from the insurance adjuster today, and the amount they quoted will barely cover building a new structure, let alone filling it with all the equipment and furniture and everything else I need to replace. And the real kicker is it's *my* fault because I never updated the policy to include all of my belongings and the new equipment I bought for the clinic."

Her voice grew shaky at the end, and I could sense her panic. And...fuck. I was trying to flip the script and be the sunshine to her gloom, but I didn't have an answer for this one.

"And then Ash called today, and this house I love is for sale, and he was going on and on about it. And about how Mom and Dad can't wait for me to move back. And Mom's already planned out the freakin' menu for when I do."

It felt like the entire floor dropped out from under me, my heart leaping into my throat at the same time my stomach dropped out of my ass.

"You're moving to Washington?" I could barely get the question out, the words like broken glass in my throat.

"No, I'm not." She paused for a second, then bit her lip, lifted a single shoulder, and blew out a heavy sigh. "Or, I don't know if I'm not. I don't know anything anymore. I don't know what I should do or where I should live. Or if Starlight Cove is right for me."

"I thought you loved it here." I thought she loved it with me.

"I do. I just... I don't know if it loves me back. I've been here for two years, and I still don't feel like I belong."

Hearing her say that, hearing the pain laced in her words, cracked my heart in two. But I didn't know what I could say to make her believe she *did* belong. That she was as much a part of Starlight Cove as me or any of my siblings, as much a part of it as Mabel with her Facebook Lives, or Esther running bingo on Mondays. That was easy for *me* to see—I'd seen it every day for the past two years, how people gravitated toward her—but I had no idea how to make her see it, too.

"Maybe moving home would be for the best," she said, her words barely a whisper, and my entire world seized up.

This was her home—*I* was her home—and it killed me that she felt like she didn't fit here. Like she'd be better somewhere else. The thought of her gone...of her moving to the other side of the country after she was finally mine was a huge, gaping wound in my chest, and I had no idea how to fix it. No idea how to make someone stay if they didn't want to.

No idea how I'd let myself fall for someone, open up completely, when this was the inevitable outcome.

"It was just a bad day," I said, as much for her as for myself. "Give it some time. Things will work out."

They had to. Because I didn't know what I'd do if they didn't.

She shot me a small smile. "Isn't that my line?"

"Yeah, which means shit's gotten real weird." And I

knew one thing that would take both our minds off everything. "How about you tell me all the reasons you love Starlight Cove while I eat your pussy?"

She blew out another laugh—this one sounding much more real—and shook her head. "Someone's got a one-track mind tonight."

"That's not a no."

She looked at me, her lip caught between her teeth, and slowly shook her head. "No, it's not."

I slid my hands up the outsides of her thighs until I gripped the sides of her panties, one brow raised. She shifted in her seat, lifting her ass up from the chair, and allowed me to pull them down her legs and off her completely. I tossed them behind me—hopefully avoiding Chuck—and pushed my T-shirt up and over her tits, exposing her to me completely.

I cupped one of her breasts in my palm and leaned forward, circling her nipple with my tongue before pulling back and blowing a gust of air against it.

"Beck," she whispered, her eyes full of heat as she watched me.

"I've got you, sunshine." I gripped her hips, tugged her to the edge of the seat, and hooked her legs over the arms of the chair, spreading her wide open for my hungry gaze. Jesus Christ, she was gorgeous, all soft and pink. I ran my nose up the inside of her thigh, inhaling deeply—her scent a mix of us both, my soap and her Everlyness, that made my mouth water, demanding a taste.

"Here's how this is going to work," I said, ghosting my breath over her pussy. "You're going to tell me all the things you love about Starlight Cove, and I'm going to lick your pussy. You don't talk, I don't lick."

"That's mean."

I shrugged. "Those are the rules. Take 'em or leave 'em."

She sighed, pulling my hat off and tossing it to the side before running her fingers through my hair. "Guess I'll take them."

I raised a brow. "Then you better start talking."

"Okay... Um...well, I love that it's on the ocean."

Humming, I pressed an openmouthed kiss to the crease of her leg and raised a brow.

She exhaled a deep breath and relaxed back into the chair. "You said you'd lick, not tease."

I licked a path up the inside of her thigh. "Never said it'd be your pussy."

Her mouth dropped open as she huffed out a gasp. "That's not fair."

"The more reasons you give, the more licking I do. Better start thinking."

Shifting her hips, she attempted to get closer to my mouth before finally giving up with a sigh. "Fine. I love that people greet me by name at the store."

Rewarding her for playing the game, I grinned and swiped a long line through her slit, licking her from her entrance to her clit before sucking it into my mouth.

She moaned, and the sound shot straight to my cock, making my already hard length throb.

I pulled back and blew a gust of air across her clit. "Keep going."

"Right. Sorry. Um... I love Mabel's Lives...usually."

She arched into me as I swirled my tongue around her clit, then sagged back on the chair with a huff when I pulled away. With a groan, she said, "What do I need to do to keep your mouth on me?"

"Just keep talking, baby."

"Oh God. Okay, I love that I don't have to lock my doors...and that I can walk on the beach at midnight...and that everyone here takes care of each other."

With each item she listed, her words got a little breathier, her sentences coming out choppy as I did as I promised and kept my mouth on her pussy. I rolled my tongue against her, sucked her clit, and slipped two fingers inside her, all while she rocked her hips against my face, seeking her pleasure.

"Fuck, you're dripping down my fingers, sunshine. You needed my mouth, didn't you?"

"Yes," she breathed, tightening her fingers in my hair as she stared down at me with hooded eyes.

"You forgot something on your list."

"What?"

"I'm here to eat this sweet cunt when you have a bad day and make you come hard enough to gush all over my tongue."

"Oh my God, Beck. *Please.*"

Glancing up at her from between her legs, I scraped my bottom teeth over her clit, and a shudder racked her body. "Tell me."

"You know you're the best part of Starlight Cove. My *favorite* part."

I hummed against her, those words filling my chest in a way that nothing else had. I was so fucking gone for this girl, and there was no way I was losing her after I'd just gotten her. So I'd give her what she needed. I'd make her come hard against my mouth before taking her to bed and reminding her why we were so perfect together.

And then I'd figure out what the fuck I needed to do to make sure she stayed in Starlight Cove, right where she belonged.

CHAPTER TWENTY-TWO

BECK

"CALL IT TWINTUITION, but it feels like this attitude you have going on is about more than just dear old Dad," Ford said as we walked back from completing our weekly delivery service.

"What gave it away?" I asked dryly.

"Oh, I don't know. Maybe it was when you kicked that puppy."

I rolled my eyes at his dramatics, but he wasn't far off. The irony was, it felt like *my* puppy had been kicked. It'd only been two days since my talk with Everly, and maybe she would eventually settle into this new rhythm, but I didn't want to wait for that to happen. I *couldn't* wait. I'd spent nearly the entirety of our relationship waiting, and I didn't want to go back to that place anymore.

I'd finally gotten to where I wasn't always anticipating

the other shoe falling, and I...enjoyed it. I'd been happy in my life for the first time in a long time, and it killed me that instead of mirroring my outlook, Everly had been feeling lost.

"Everly's thinking about moving back to Washington."

Ford jerked to a stop in the middle of the winding road that led through the resort. "What the fuck? Since when?"

I took off my hat and scrubbed a hand through my hair before settling the cap back on my head. "I don't know how long she's been thinking about it. She just told me on Monday."

"What happened on Monday?"

"What *didn't* happen on Monday?"

"Gonna need a little more than that, man."

I blew out a heavy sigh. "She'd had a really bad day. The first day of house calls didn't go great, she can't drive a stick shift to save her life, she forgot the lunch I made her, and Esther booked an appointment for her cat *while* she was at the senior center for bingo—who does that, by the way?—and didn't bother to tell Everly. So Everly, who was already running behind, showed up at her house and, *surprise*, Esther wasn't there. And now Everly's thinking *she's* the odd one out because she doesn't know every fucking movement of every fucking resident of Starlight Cove. She doesn't think she belongs here. Doesn't think she fits in. And I don't know how to tell her that the people in town orbit around her like she's the goddamn sun when she can't see it for herself."

Ford's eyes grew wider the more I spoke. He glanced around at the various guests roaming the property—that was something we hadn't had to contend with for years—and tugged me off the beaten path and toward the beach. It was cooler out today, with a storm settling in, and waves crashed against the shore, the ocean's turmoil mirroring my own.

"Okay, first of all, I think that's more than you've said at once in your entire life. Second, it's not going to help anybody if you lose your shit."

I blew out a humorless laugh, dropped down onto the sand, and braced my forearms on my bent knees. "I'm in love with her, Ford. If she leaves..."

Fuck, I didn't want to think about what it'd be like if she left. What my life would be reduced to. Couldn't even remember what Starlight Cove was before she'd shown up. Before she'd swept into the diner with her way-too-fuck-ing-chirpy-for-7-a.m. voice and her smile that shot straight through my heart and her Everly Voodoo that'd had me wrapped around her finger in less time than it took me to make her favorite grilled cheese.

Ford sat next to me, bracing himself back on his hands and stretching his legs out in front of him. "Does she know that?"

"Everyone else in the whole fucking town seems to. How could she not?"

"Okay, but did you tell her? Or did you just grunt at her like you usually do?"

Well, I'd made her come three times last night, and again this morning in the shower, but somehow, I didn't think that was what he was getting at.

"I'll take that as a no," he said.

"What am I supposed to do? Just drop the bomb *now*? Tell her I love her after she's already told me she's thinking of leaving? She'll think it's a ploy to get her to stay."

"It *is* a ploy to get her to stay."

"You know what I mean. Everyone's always forced her into her decisions. Hell, she's *here* because her aunt died and gave her the clinic. If that hadn't happened, where would she be?" The thought sent a sharp ache through my heart, my gut churning over the very real possibility that I never would've known her. "It's not fair of me to rope her into something if she doesn't really want it."

"Wow." He stared at me, brows raised. "Well, that's super noble and shit, but this is your happiness we're talking about too. I get that you don't want to corner her, but that's not all this is about. You can't tell me a part of you isn't hesitating because you're scared."

I looked straight ahead, lips pressed together in a thin line, because fuck yes, I was scared. I'd never in my life had something so important to lose, and now I had *everything* to lose.

"Look, I know Dad fucked us all up," he said, "but at some point, you've gotta make the decision on if you want to let that steer the rest of your life, or if you want to take control and not let a man who's spent the past ten years locked away in a single-room cottage instead of actually living be the one running your life."

I let his words sink in, the certainty of them ringing true. "That's pretty deep for you. You following some new influencers or what?"

"Nah." He shrugged. "It's the romances. I didn't realize they could go so deep and not just, you know, *deep*."

I breathed out a laugh and rubbed the heels of my palms against my eyes. "Believe me, I know. Everly's already given me an entire dissertation on how romance novels are inherently feminist and help heal traumas in healthy ways. And, you know, they're hot as hell."

He laughed along with me, quiet descending between us. Ford and I truly could not have been more opposite, but we knew each other. We *got* each other. And the silence between us always felt as comfortable as if I were alone.

Eventually, he nudged me with his elbow. "This is where she wants to be, man. She's happy here. She's happy with *you*. And whether or not she's told you, she loves you back. God knows why," he said dryly, "but she does."

"Maybe. But that still doesn't solve the issues she's facing. Even if she miraculously decided to stay, that doesn't take care of the fact that she's not going to have enough from insurance to rebuild a home and a business here. The entire reason she came is gone."

"Well, then it sounds like you need to give her a reason to stay."

"Great, how do I do that?"

"Fuck if I know."

I huffed out a laugh and shook my head. "You're no help."

"Did you think I'd be? You came to the wrong McKenzie."

Images of our sister, tackling any situation head on with no concern for things like helmets, flicked through my mind, and I scrubbed a hand down my face. "Fuck."

"Yeah, fuck. This should be fun..."

I stared out at the ocean that'd been our backyard my entire life. This had been my home for thirty-two years, but it hadn't felt like it until Everly had come into my life. She'd brought sunshine and happiness and *hope*. And I would do anything to keep her.

"You sure you want to enlist the dictator with this?" Ford asked.

"Could possibly be my worst idea ever." I stood, offering Ford a hand to help him to his feet. "But I don't think I have a choice."

Everly

I'D ALWAYS BEEN lucky in my life in that things tended to come easily for me. Or maybe it was just that I tended to choose the path of least resistance. From the time I was little, I didn't usually put up a fight. One, because most of the time, it wasn't worth it. But probably even more so because I didn't want to give anyone a reason to discard me or write me off.

I already felt like I was on uneven footing, even though my parents had never done anything to make me feel that way. I'd gotten it in my head from a very young age that the way to be the best daughter—the best person—I could be was to just go along with it. If I was served something I didn't like, I ate it with a smile because I didn't want to be any hassle. If I was put in an extracurricular activity I didn't enjoy, I stuck it out without a peep. I'd never pushed back on anything in my life. And I'd enjoyed that life. It was nice, and I didn't have many complaints.

But what would my life be like if I wasn't so busy pleasing everyone else other than myself?

I'd had a glimpse of what that would be like since I'd moved here. Because although the reasons I'd come to Starlight Cove in the first place were based on someone else's design of my life, my life here was *mine*. And for some reason, Beck had been the one person I'd been completely and totally myself with. I didn't sugarcoat anything with him. If I had a bad day, he saw it. He knew I hated brussels sprouts and I secretly loved raunchy comedies and that I loathed softball even though I'd played it all through high school at my parents' urging.

From the beginning, we'd had a connection. Even when he'd spent the majority of the time responding to me in nothing but grunts, I'd just felt like there was something there.

But now, when everything else was crumbling, it felt like even we were on rocky ground. I was basically living with him, but even still, there were some days when I didn't see him until he crawled into bed next to me. I knew this was just a phase like anything else, but I hated it.

He was busy helping with the Cupcake Festival, which was apparently something that happened every year at this time. That meant this would be my third, and yet I had no recollection of it at all. Maybe Ash really was onto something when he said I was oblivious.

One thing I couldn't miss was how weird everyone had been acting lately. People were actively going out of their way to avoid me when they saw me around town, and it was getting harder and harder to convince myself that this was where I belonged.

I unlocked Beck's apartment door and strode inside. And though I knew it would be empty, it still sucked to have that confirmed when Chuckanut was the only one greeting me. Well, that and a shit-ton of Post-it notes.

Beck and I had seen each other so little in the past week and a half that we'd taken to communicating through them. They were scattered around the apartment, most of his reminding me to eat or lock the door or turn off the stove. And mine to him revolved almost entirely around how cute his butt was because I figured it'd make him smile since I wasn't there to do it in person.

He'd left me three tonight, all of them arrows pointing directly to the fridge where he'd left my dinner, complete with reheating instructions like the saint he was.

I didn't know how such a huge shift in our relationship could have happened in such a short amount of time. Had it really only been three weeks ago when I'd been living on my own and totally unaware of how amazing my best friend was?

But no...I hadn't been unaware of it. I *knew* how amazing he was. I just hadn't known how amazing he was for *me*.

I'd just settled in Beck's chair with my plate full of deliciousness when my cell phone rang, my mom calling right on time. She hadn't missed a day since the fire. Hadn't missed a coercion attempt to get me to move home either.

I hated that my stomach was in knots every time I saw her name on my screen. Hated the thought that she obviously wasn't happy with my life here. Hated the thought of disappointing her.

I took a deep breath and answered. "Hey, Mom."

"Guess who's back in town?" she said without preamble. "Mallory's son, you remember him? Mark? He's a few years older than you...a *doctor*...and he's looking to settle down."

I closed my eyes with a sigh and pressed my head back into the chair. "That's great, Mom, but he sounds a little young for you. And there's that whole you're already married thing to worry about."

My mom gasped. "Heavens no, Evie. I mean for *you*."

"Well, it's been a long time since I've seen Mark, so I can't be sure, but I'm guessing he'll probably want a local wife."

"That's why it's so perfect! It's just one more reason for you to move home."

My stomach churned, but I couldn't tell anymore if it was over the thought of staying or leaving. "I'd really like to talk about something other than me moving, so why don't you tell me what's new? How is quilting club?"

After I steered her in the direction of one of her favorite topics, she prattled on for ten minutes, barely taking a breath as she detailed their upcoming projects for the children's hospital.

And though I'd asked her if we could stop talking about my moving back, she couldn't help but drop one last comment as we were saying our goodbyes. "I know Ash told you about that house on Maple Street that went up for sale. I just drove by it today, and there's a price reduced sticker on the sign!"

"Mom, you do know I live in Maine, right?"

"Well, *now* you do, but this is just something to keep in your pocket for the future."

A future I wasn't so sure of anymore.

After we said our goodbyes, I stared down at the plate full of food I hadn't taken a single bite of. In the twenty minutes we'd been talking, I'd lost my appetite. But Beck had worked so hard on my dinner, so I forced myself to eat a bit before I covered the plate and put it back into the fridge.

Chuckanut was curled on the ostentatious bed Beck had purchased her, dead to the world, and it was too quiet in the apartment without his presence. Wanting to feel close to him, I climbed out on the roof and sat, my knees tucked up to my chest, and I listened to the waves against the shore.

I didn't know what to do. Didn't know if I should stay or if I should go. I couldn't even parse my feelings on it anymore, half of me yearning for familiarity and the comfort that I knew home would provide. And the other half of me wanting to explore this new side of myself, this newfound life that I'd built all on my own without anyone's input. One that included Beck.

Still, my mom's words rang in the back of my mind as I pulled out my phone and searched for the house I'd loved for years. It was still as gorgeous as I remembered, a single story in a soft, cheery yellow with white shutters, flower boxes under the front windows, and a porch swing I'd always pictured I'd sit on with my future husband.

Except I couldn't picture that anymore. Now, it was just me, there by myself.

With the price cut, it was now just under the amount

the insurance adjuster quoted me. Maybe that was a sign to move back home. Maybe it was meant to be.

But there was only one problem with that. Beck wasn't in Washington. And I wasn't so sure I could live without him.

CHAPTER TWENTY-THREE

BECK

I COULDN'T BELIEVE we'd pulled it off. In less than two weeks, we'd put together a fully functioning festival, complete with vendors, entertainment, and even an auction to raise funds. And all of it was going to Everly. As soon as I'd enlisted Addison's help, it'd been a whirlwind. She'd whipped the town into a frenzy, and everyone had been all too ready and willing to do whatever was needed to help Everly, exactly how I knew they would. I just wished she could see it.

If these past ten days had taught me anything, it was that I couldn't handle being away from her, and yet I was still getting my fix every night. There was no way I was going to let her move to Washington. At least, not without me.

Yes, this festival was to show her all of Starlight Cove adored her, and yes, I'd had plans drawn up for a house-slash-business—that just so happened to fit perfectly on an unused section of the resort property—but in the end, it was her choice. If she decided to take the money and move back to Washington, I wasn't going to stop her.

But I *would* be going with her.

There was no me without Everly.

She'd brought out the best in me, found a crack in the wall I'd surrounded myself with and slipped inside. Then sat right down beside me like she'd always been there.

I was tired of living in fear. Tired of perpetually anticipating the worst-case scenario—and not just preparing for it, but counting on it.

Everly was the best this world had to offer, and somehow, some way, she'd become mine. And tonight, I was going to lay that all out for her.

"I really can't believe I've never heard of this festival before." Everly leaned close, her hand encased in mine as she glanced around at the Cupcake Festival we'd put together in a matter of days. "I feel like I've been living under a rock."

I cleared my throat, forcing back the cringe because I hated that this was probably making her feel even more left out, but it was only for a few more hours. And after nearly two weeks of watching my every move and protecting this secret, I wasn't about to blow it now.

The same couldn't be said for the rest of the Starlight Cove residents enjoying the festivities. The only way we'd been able to get the town to agree to secrecy was to promise them a year of free coffee and a free meal—on a date of their choosing...Mabel was adamant about that—at the diner. Besides an offhanded remark from Everly asking if it was just her or if everyone in town was suddenly acting sketchy, I didn't think she'd noticed.

Now, though, it'd be impossible for her not to. Every single person who walked by glanced between us, then down to our joined hands, then not so subtly shot me a wink, all while grinning like idiots. Every. Single. Person.

By the time we'd made our way through most of the festival, gorging ourselves on cupcakes, and headed toward the lawn where a band was set up in front of the gazebo, I was sure every resident in Starlight Cove had blown our cover.

"Why is everyone winking at you like they know you're about to get laid?" Everly turned to me, her brows raised. "Are we acting out Chapter Twelve, and you decided to tell everyone else but me?"

Sweet fucking Christ, this woman was going to kill me. There was nothing I wanted more than to take her to some dark alcove and fuck her outside, my hand capturing all those sweet moans that were just for me. But that would probably be a bad idea since I was the one who'd put on this whole thing. Though, who was going to know?

With a groan, I tugged her behind a huge tree and pressed her up against it, caging her in. I lowered my face, brushing my lips against hers before sucking her bottom one into my mouth. "You are too fucking tempting, you know that?"

"Yeah?" She tucked her fingers into the waistband of my jeans, so close to my already-straining cock. "You going to do something about that?"

I glanced out at the festivities going on around us, then down at Everly's dress—easy access—then up to her eyes, finding the same hunger reflected in them as I was sure shone in mine. "Hell yes, I am. But we gotta be—"

"There you are," Addison called from far too fucking close for my liking, considering the monster hard-on I was rocking.

"Fuck." I dropped my forehead to Everly's shoulder as I tried to will my cock down.

She breathed out a laugh, running her hands through my hair. "Are things a little...hard for you right now?"

"Very funny."

"I thought so."

"What are you doing?" Addison asked, stopping right next to us. "It's your turn."

Thankfully, my cock was mostly behaved, so I stepped back, grabbing Everly's hand as we faced my sister. "My turn for what?"

"The auction, obviously." The *bachelor* auction she'd sworn would be the biggest fundraiser of them all because, and I quote, "There are a lot of horny old women in this town, and I'm not above exploiting that."

"What about it?"

She shot me a look that was both imploring and scary as hell. "You're up."

I sure as hell was *not* up because I was not a bachelor. We might not have said the words, but I was Everly's, plain and simple. "No, I don't think I am."

"*Yes*, you are," she said through gritted teeth, a forced smile on her face. "Remember that *thing* we're raising money for?"

"Yes."

"Well, you want all the money we can get, right?"

I clenched my jaw so tightly, I wouldn't be surprised if Everly could hear my teeth grinding. "Yes."

"Great!" she said with false brightness. "Then get up there and give these people whatever it is they find so enticing about you. Personally, I don't see it."

"Well, I should hope not. You're my sister."

"You've got five minutes, or I'm making you go out there shirtless." And with that, the little witch walked toward the gazebo where a line of guys stood waiting their turn.

"So..." Everly said. "You're auctioning yourself off?"

"I wasn't aware I was." I scrubbed a hand down my face and exhaled a heavy sigh. I could think of twelve thousand things I'd rather do than auction myself off for the "horny old women" of Starlight Cove, despite the cause we were raising money for. "I've gotta go talk to her."

"Oh. Sure, okay," she said, surprise and...hurt? evident in her voice. *Fuck.* I was going to kill Addison for this. "I'll just...hang out and watch the crowd go wild until you're...done."

"I'm just going to go tell her to find someone else, okay?" I cupped Everly's face, brushing my thumb across her lower lip. I couldn't tell her yet what this festival was for or why Addison was pushing for every dollar we could get. So instead, I leaned in and kissed her, brushing my tongue against hers and pouring everything I felt into it. Saying without words how much she meant to me. How much I loved her. How every bit of this was for her.

Everly

WELL, tonight certainly hadn't gone how I thought it would.

Finally, Beck and I had been able to connect, when it'd been nothing but hit or miss for almost two weeks. I missed him fiercely, and that in and of itself was what had made my decision so easy.

Besides the fact that I'd grown to love this life I'd carved out for myself here, I couldn't move back home to Washington because Beck wasn't there, and I'd be miserable without him.

I'd even told my parents as much earlier today. I'd called them and finally laid it all on the line, telling them that I loved them and I missed them but that my life was here now. It'd been unnerving, but as soon as the words had come out of my mouth, I could hear the truth in them. It was as if a giant weight had been lifted off my chest, and I could finally breathe again. Why the hell hadn't I been standing up for myself all the time?

As I was telling them all the reasons I wanted to stay, I'd realized I loved this life I'd built here in Starlight Cove because it was *mine*. And maybe the reason I hadn't felt like I belonged here like I did in my hometown had more to do with the fact that I wasn't bending over backward to please everyone else and instead was focusing more on my own happiness. And I was totally and completely okay with that. It was time for a little selfishness.

So after my stellar afternoon when I'd finally made the decision to stick around and figure out how I was going to make the amount of insurance money I was getting work, now I was facing my boyfriend auctioning himself off for a date with someone else.

Okay, so we'd never had the boyfriend/girlfriend discussion, but I'd assumed since we were sleeping in the same bed and he spent most nights inside me, that meant we were sort of a thing. And if we were sort of a thing, I really wasn't all that excited about the possibility of him going out on a date—or whatever it was they were auctioning off—with another person. Especially the hungry-looking vultures surrounding me. Actually, even if we weren't a thing, I really wasn't all that excited about it.

While I watched Beck and Addison facing off in a

yelling match—I was too far away to hear what they were saying, but their body language spoke volumes—I made my way toward the gazebo. And then, because I was a masochist, apparently, there I stood as they auctioned off bachelor after bachelor, my stomach knotting tighter with each one that passed.

Since I was close enough to the melee, Addison joined me after a while, and we watched as people threw more money at the bachelors than I'd expected—anywhere between a couple hundred up to almost a thousand for Levi. The bad boy of the McKenzie brood stood in the gazebo, arms crossed and face a mask of disinterest as the bids kept flying.

"You must have some sort of magic over your brothers," I said to Addison. "First Beck, and now Levi? How'd you get them to agree?"

She waved a hand through the air. "You don't need to worry about Beck. Just a little prearranged opportunity that's going to go for megabucks. As for Levi, I gave him three free passes to skip family meetings to be used at his discretion."

"Wow. You guys really went all out for this. What's the cause again?" I asked, realizing now that I hadn't seen any flyers about it whatsoever.

"What's that? Oh, sorry, looks like they need me back there! I'll catch up with you later, okay?" Addison said before scurrying off toward the gazebo where only a few more men stood, Beck among them.

And yeah, I didn't care what this "prearranged opportunity" was. It was with my boyfriend—whether he knew it or not—and I wasn't having it.

The closer it got to his turn, the tighter the knot grew in my stomach. He was clearly not happy with it, his face set in a grim line, arms crossed and jaw clenched while Ford propped an arm on his shoulder, laughing like he was having the time of his life. I couldn't sit by and watch someone else bid on him, but since I hadn't exactly expected this, I only had twenty-three dollars in my purse. Hopefully they'd take an IOU or let me run to the ATM so I could cash out.

Finally, it was Beck's turn, and he stepped up—or rather, Addison shoved him up. He stood in the gazebo, looking about as excited to be there as Levi had. He wore his usual uniform of a T-shirt and jeans, but gone was his standard backward baseball cap. Instead, his hair hung loosely, the tousled locks hanging over his forehead, and my fingers itched to push it back. Itched to wipe that look off his face. Itched to remind him he was mine and I was his and, together, we were everything.

From the beginning, his entire persona should have put me off. We were opposites in every way, but somehow, we'd connected and it'd felt inevitable. Like magnets clicking together. I hadn't realized it then, but that first day when I'd stepped foot into the diner, everything had slotted into place. It was the beginning of my new life. A new life I'd created for myself—it wasn't perfect and it wasn't easy, but it was mine. And the only thing I needed in it, without question, was him.

"Our next bachelor is none other than Beck McKenzie. You probably know him best for serving the greatest coffee in Starlight Cove, not to mention those amazing blueberry scones." The auctioneer gave an exaggerated wink to the crowd. "I think we all know why we're here, and you'll get it. Don't let that scowl fool you! Beneath the angry glower is a sweet man who would do *anything* for those important to him, and I think tonight is proof enough of that."

The bidding started then and grew rapidly. So rapidly, I hadn't had a chance to jump in before another bid was tossed out. And another and another.

"Your man is quite the draw," Mabel said, stepping up to my side.

"What?" I asked distractedly, sliding my eyes to hers before moving them back to watch two ladies—one of whom was Charlotte, the beautiful woman from the bank Beck had sweet-talked for me. "Sorry, Mabel, I can't really talk right now."

"It's very sweet, what he's doing. Don't you think?" She elbowed me in the side again. "After the *you know what* that I'm not allowed to talk to you about."

It was then that I noticed she was pointing her phone in my direction, clearly filming a Facebook Live.

"Going once," the auctioneer called, and I snapped my head around.

I shot my hand up to bid, only the problem was I

hadn't heard what the last amount was, so I shouted the first number that came to mind. "Five hundred dollars!"

Mabel gasped beside me and tugged on my shirt sleeve. "What are you doing?"

"Bidding," I said. I narrowed my eyes at the cougar from the bank and dared her to bid against me.

Apparently, I needed to work on my stink eye, because she raised her hand to increase the bid, and I swore under my breath.

"But you can't bid!" Mabel hissed.

I raised my hand to up the bid again, trying my hardest to ignore Mabel, which wasn't easy, considering she was a distraction just by breathing.

"It totally defeats the purpose!" she said. "You can't bid on your own stuff to help your own thing!"

"What?" Exasperated, I turned my attention to her, having no clue what she was talking about.

"I didn't— I mean, it's just—" Mabel stumbled over her words, shaking her head and trying to backtrack. And in the ten seconds she'd had my undivided attention, the bidding must've continued, because suddenly, a gavel sounded.

"Sold, to Charlotte," the auctioneer called.

"Fuck," I said under my breath, my shoulders slumping.

"Oh dear. That is definitely not family-friendly. I'm just gonna scooch," Mabel said. "But don't worry, sugar. He's just auctioning off a little piece of deliciousness." And then she scurried off into the crowd like she hadn't totally ruined my plan.

Yeah, a little piece of deliciousness that was all mine.

I'd just lost the man I was absolutely, unequivocally, head over heels in love with to a beautiful older woman. A woman who'd probably lived in Starlight Cove her whole life and didn't forget things like shutting off her curling iron, and probably didn't need a keeper because she remembered to eat three meals a day, and she also no doubt knew how to drive a stick. So that was just fantastic. A cherry on top of my shit sundae.

"Everly." Quinn stepped up next to me, sounding slightly out of breath. "Hey."

"Hey, Quinn," I answered distractedly, my eyes focused on Beck where he stood, arms crossed and scowl firmly in place. He scanned the crowd, his gaze landing on me. His face softened and he dropped his arms, taking a step in my direction before Addison and Charlotte blocked his path.

"How are you feeling?" she asked, and I focused on her, desperate for the distraction because I couldn't watch him make date arrangements with another woman.

It took me a minute to realize she wasn't asking how I felt about the man I was in love with going out on a date with someone else and that she was actually talking about the life-changing fire I'd been in that'd set off this entire thing.

"Oh, fine. Well, as fine as I can be. I'm still trying to get everything in order, but I'll figure it out."

"I'm so glad to hear that."

"How about you?"

She blew out a heavy sigh and shook her head. "Honestly? Really damn tired of misogynistic old men."

A surprised laugh gusted out of me. "One of those days, huh?"

"One of those *years*. All I want to do is go home, take a bath, and have a glass of wine."

"That sounds amazing, but it's a far cry from a festival. What're you doing here?"

"It's my master plan to get in the good graces of said misogynistic old man." She shrugged and tipped her head toward the gazebo. "I thought maybe throwing some money toward a Starlight Cove cause might shine a light in my favor. I'm just glad I made it before this was over. But who knows? Maybe I'll meet my future husband."

I cringed because there was only one bachelor left, and she wasn't going to like who it was.

"What's that face for?" she asked.

"Um, well—"

"And the last bachelor up for auction tonight is none other than Starlight Cove's favorite flirt, Ford McKenzie. You know him best for shooting a salacious grin and a wink your way, but he's also good with his hands, if you know what I mean."

"You've got to be kidding me," Quinn said under her breath. She closed her eyes and tipped her head back, repeating over and over, "This is for the greater good, this is for the greater good..."

"Anything that'll stick it to a misogynist," I agreed.

"I need to look on the bright side. I already went out with a guy who took me to the McDonald's drive-thru before sneaking me into his parents' basement—that was just last month, by the way—so surely a date with Ford can't be any worse than that. Right?"

"Probably not?" I said, though it came out as more of a question.

Still, Quinn squared her shoulders, faced the gazebo, and totally obliterated every other bid when she called out, "Two thousand dollars."

The auctioneer stared in our direction, openmouthed and frozen for half a second—the look mirrored on Ford's face—before shaking herself out of it and slamming the gavel. "Sold!"

Quinn was two thousand dollars poorer and leaving with a date to a guy she didn't want anything to do with. Meanwhile, I was leaving with the same twenty-three dollars I'd come in with, but I hadn't won the one thing I desperately wanted more than anything else.

CHAPTER TWENTY-FOUR

BECK

AT SOME POINT between glaring daggers at my sister and delivering on the six-hundred-dollar auction bid, I'd lost sight of Everly. The festival was winding down with only a few stragglers left. Thankfully, my meddling, no-good—and, yeah, amazing—sister was handling the wrap-up so I could finally come clean to Everly, and I was so ready. I was tired of keeping shit from her and wanted her to know how much this town loved her. How everyone had jumped at the chance to help.

I was still pissed at Addison for blindsiding me with the auction block, and I'd only relented after she'd assured me that everyone bidding did so knowing they were *only* bidding for my blueberry scone recipe and nothing else. Well, everyone but Everly. None of us had seen that twist coming, but I couldn't deny how my dick got hard at her jealousy over me, even if there was absolutely no reason for it.

I could've been surrounded by a million supermodels, and I'd still only have eyes for my sunshine.

I'd just finished wrapping up a string of lights when someone shoved me in my back. Though it hadn't been particularly hard, I stumbled forward, caught off guard, and glanced behind me.

"You're not going on a date with her." Everly stood, hands on hips, her mouth set in a flat line. "I don't care that she's beautiful and her boobs are bigger than mine, and I don't care that she's older and more experienced and has probably already acted out Chapter Eight, not to mention Twenty-Two and Thirty and Ten, so she could show you a thing or two. Or that she probably remembers to eat all her meals and knows how to drive a stick and has an actual home and belongings and doesn't wear borrowed leggings and her boyfriend's old T-shirts. I don't want you to go out on a date with her."

My brows inched higher up my forehead with each impassioned word that left her lips, and holy *shit*, I wasn't sure I'd ever wanted her more. I glanced around, noticing my sister paying way too much attention to us and a suspicious Mabel hovering far too close for my liking, so I tugged Everly behind a closed-up food cart to give us a modicum of privacy.

"There's that word again," I said.

"What?" she snapped.

"Boyfriend."

Everly huffed and glared at me. "Did you hear anything else I said?"

"Yes." I nodded, fighting the urge to push her up against the cart and show her exactly how much I didn't care about another woman and exactly how much I loved when she claimed me as hers.

"Well, are you going to say anything about it?"

"I'd rather use my mouth for other things, but if you need the words, fine." I leaned back against the cart, spreading my legs wide and tugging her to stand between them until her body was pressed against mine. "I'm going to have to take your word for it on her boobs because yours are the only tits I'm looking at. I don't care how much experience she has, because I'd much rather explore Chapters Ten and Twenty-Two and especially Thirty with *you*. I fucking love when you wear my clothes—especially where everyone can see it. Let everyone know you're mine." Something flared in her eyes, but I had one last sticking point I needed her very aware of. "And I'm not going out on a date. I just want to help clean up a bit before we head home." My lips twitched at the word— something she'd been calling it for weeks. Now, I just needed to make it permanent.

"I know you're not going on a date *now*," she said. "But that very nice woman who I wish was a bit more of a harpy so I could hate her just paid hundreds of dollars to go out with you, and I don't care what I have to do. I don't care if I have to scrimp and save, if I have to eat ramen every day for six months, or if I have to steal pennies from the wishing fountain to cover it. I'm buying her out, because you are not going out on a date with her."

"You're right, sunshine. I'm not going out on a date with her."

"No, I'm not going to—" She froze, blinking up at me in surprise. "Wait. What?"

I reached out, brushing my thumb over her bottom lip. "Everyone knew they were only bidding on me for my blueberry scone recipe."

"Your blueberry—" Everly stared up at me with wide eyes. "You mean she didn't want sex?"

I huffed out a laugh and shook my head. "Jesus, no. And I wouldn't give a shit if she did because I'm not interested in anyone else. It's been you for a long time, sunshine." I cupped her face, my thumbs brushing softly against her cheeks, and leaned close, my voice just a soft rumble between us. "As much as I love this jealous side of you, there's no need for it. Did you already forget who fucked you to sleep last night and who was inside you this morning? I sort of assumed that meant I was already spoken for."

Her cheeks bloomed at my words, her eyes sparkling as she stared up at me, hands pressed to my chest. "You are?"

I kissed her, just a soft press of my lips on hers, before pulling back. "I sure as hell hope so. I'm yours. And I thought I made my intentions clear with this festival."

"With the— What? *You* did all this? Why?"

The same reason I did anything. "For you."

She shook her head, eyes searching mine. "I don't understand."

"I—"

"This is my time to shine!" Mabel called as she popped out from behind a tree, phone held above her head as she shuffled toward us. "That was all very sweet, but I've got something you need to watch, sugar!"

I groaned, dropping my head back to the cart behind me and closing my eyes. Couldn't get a moment's peace around here. "Jesus, it better not be what you *accidentally* showed me earlier today, Mabel." I shuddered, remembering her "instructional" video for the products she sold. Fortunately, there were clothes involved, but if I never had to see her holding a ten-inch lifelike dildo again, it'd be too soon.

"Oh, it was just a fake penis, Beck," she chided, rolling her eyes. "Honestly, I don't understand why you're so squeamish about it. You've been walking around with one for over thirty years. I'd think you'd be used to them by now."

I closed my eyes, pinching the bridge of my nose. "What do you need, Mabel? We're kind of in the middle of something."

"Right, the video. Yes, here we are."

Mabel held the phone toward us, showing a choppy video that was most definitely shot by her. It was a compilation spread out over the ten days it'd taken to put the festival together. Everything from its inception—Addison, Ford, and me at the diner, our heads together as we came up with the plan—to businesses pitching in with baskets for raffles and restaurant owners donating meals and residents setting up everything, all while keeping it from the one person it was for.

Everly's eyes were glued to the phone, but I kept my gaze on her, watching as a variety of emotions flickered over her face—shock, then awe, then happiness and gratitude. And this time when she cried, I knew they were happy tears.

Still, I cupped her face, sweeping them away with my thumbs. "See? For you. It's always for you."

"Beck," she said, her voice breaking. "I can't believe you did this."

"It's really happening, folks," Mabel whispered into her phone. "Beck and Everly are about to officially become Beverly, and you're seeing it first right here on Mabel's Lives."

Everly choked out a laugh, and I clenched my jaw, closing my eyes as I pressed our foreheads together. "Can I tell her to fuc—"

"Um, some privacy, please, Mabel?" she said, cutting me off.

"Well." She huffed. "I expect that from him, but from Starlight Cove's very own sunshine?"

"She's not Starlight Cove's sunshine, she's *my*

sunshine," I said. "And if you don't get out of here, I'm taking your phone again."

She pursed her lips and swatted a hand through the air. "Oh, you're no fun."

I just raised a brow at her, and she turned around, stalking off and finally giving Everly and me some privacy.

"So it *wasn't* my imagination that everyone was acting so strange."

My lips twitched, and I shook my head. "They're definitely not going to win any Oscars, but they were good sports."

"They were amazing." She tucked her fingers into the waistband of my jeans and leaned closer, resting her body against mine. "*You* are amazing. I'll never be able to thank you for this."

"I didn't do it for the thanks. I did it for you. You work so hard, trying to please everyone else, so I wanted to be selfish for you. That means every penny we raised is yours to do whatever you want with. None of it chains you to Starlight Cove. If you want to up and move back home to Washington and build a business there, you can."

"You'd...be okay with me leaving?" she asked, apprehension tinged in her voice.

"Fuck no. But I am right now because I already made the decision that I'd go with you."

"You would?"

"If you said the word, I'd do it in a heartbeat." I pressed a kiss to her lips. "It doesn't matter where in the world you are. You're my home and I'm yours and that's just how it is."

She bit her lip, her eyes brimming with that sparkle that'd been missing for so long. "And what if I decide this is where I want to be? What if I want to rebuild in Starlight Cove?"

A smile crept across my lips as I pulled out my phone. I thumbed to the photo of the plans I'd had drawn up and turned it toward her. Her gaze danced over the screen, no doubt taking in the drawn replica of her yellow dream house, just on a larger, two-story scale, complete with white shutters, flower boxes on the windows, and a front porch swing that faced the ocean. Her smile only grew as she took in all the small features I'd made sure were included—like the window over the kitchen sink that'd look out onto the ocean instead of a parking lot, and huge closets unlike the tiny ones at her aunt's, and enough bedrooms that we could grow into it and stay there the rest of our lives.

"And I might have already bookmarked a plot of land on the resort for such a thing," I said.

Her eyes brightened, and she threw her arms around my neck, hugging me tight. And I couldn't do anything but tuck my face into the crook of her neck and breathe her in. My Everly. My sunshine.

"Is that a yes?"

She laughed, her breath ghosting over my neck. "It's a hell yes."

CHAPTER TWENTY-FIVE

EVERLY

EVEN IN MY WILDEST DAYDREAMS, I couldn't have pictured a scene as perfect as this.

The following evening, Beck and I walked to a part of the resort I ran by every morning—a place I'd felt connected to from the beginning. A place that would be perfect for the clinic and my dream home. Well, *our* dream home. It had a beautiful beach and enough foliage to give the illusion of privacy. In reality, we were only a five-minute walk from the diner and another five to the main inn.

In the exact place where our future porch swing would be, I sat in the cradle of Beck's thighs, his legs bent, arms wrapped around me as we stared out at the ocean in the fading sunlight, the waves lapping softly against the shore.

It was…serenity. Pure and utter perfection. And it was ours.

"So, how long have you been planning this for?" I asked.

He pressed a kiss to my temple and tightened his arms around me. "Not long. I never allowed myself to dream with you, sunshine."

There wasn't a trace of teasing in his voice, so I tipped my head back to stare up at him. "Why not?"

He shrugged against me. "I didn't think you were meant to be mine."

I grinned, pressing a kiss to the underside of his jaw, his short beard tickling my lips. "Well, the joke's on you, because now you're stuck with me."

"I think it's the other way around." He ducked his head, burying his face in the crook of my neck before pressing a kiss there. Against my skin, he asked, "Are you really sure about this?"

"Are you?"

He huffed out a laugh. "Sunshine, I've been yours since the day you spilled coffee down the front of my shirt."

I furrowed my brow, trying to remember when I'd done that. I hadn't spilled coffee in— I gasped. "Wait...that was, like, a year and a half ago."

He just hummed against my skin, the vibration sending a delicious shiver down my spine.

"Seriously? A year and a half?"

"Seriously. A year and a half."

My stomach flipped, the thought of this man wanting

me for that long, of him witnessing every bad hair day and lapse in judgment and bout of PMS and loving me quietly the whole time, sending a burst of warmth through me. "I thought you could barely tolerate me."

"I've been in love with you for a long time. Your brother can be an ass, but he's not wrong about you being oblivious."

I snorted. "Yeah, I'm starting to realize that."

"I'm telling you right now, if any other man comes around and tries to feed you, take care of your dog for you, or makes you text him when you get home after ensuring your safety, he and I are going to have a very long, very painful chat."

I laughed and shifted, turning around to face him and straddle his lap. Draping my arms over his shoulders, I shook my head. "Don't worry, I think your grumbly face will scare anyone else away." I bit my lip, all teasing gone from my tone. "And I love you, too."

His eyes heated as he slipped his hands under the hem of my T-shirt, resting them on my bare back, his touch something I wasn't sure I'd ever get used to. Wasn't sure I ever wanted to. Voice low, he said, "Say it again."

I smiled at the subtle bark of a command in his voice. "I love you."

He pressed a kiss to my jaw. "Again."

I exhaled a sigh, tipping my head to the side to allow him more room. "I love you, Beck."

He groaned, cupping my face and kissing me with pent-up desire like we hadn't fucked like bunnies when we'd gotten home last night and like he hadn't already made me come just this morning.

After long moments, he finally pulled back, sliding his hands down to my back once again. "You didn't answer me. Are you sure about this?"

I could read this sincerity in his eyes, the uncertainty still there, and I wanted nothing more than to erase it completely. To reassure him there was nowhere else I wanted to be—no one else I wanted to share my life with than him. I shifted against him, sliding closer as I pressed my lips to his. "I've never been more sure of anything in my life than I am of you."

He groaned against my mouth, clenching his fingers at my back. "Sunshine... You can't say shit like that, grind your pussy down on me, and not expect to get fucked."

Okay, so he wasn't the only one with some pent-up desire...

"What if that's exactly what I'm expecting?" I asked right before I kissed him, slowly rocking against where he was already thick and ready for me.

His grip on me tightened, and I gasped when he shifted me harder against him, the thin material of my panties doing nothing to disguise the stiff bulge of his cock. "Is that why you wore this sexy little skirt? Finally wanted me to Chapter Twelve you?"

I breathed out a laugh even as my body heated at the thought of him taking me out here in the open where anyone could see. True, we were far away from any cottages and on the other side of the resort property from the main inn. But still, the path meandered this way, and the guests were known to roam, especially at sunset.

"With all the teasing, I'm beginning to think you aren't going to put your money where your mouth is," I said.

"I'll put my mouth anywhere you want it."

I bit my lip and shifted in his lap. My nipples tingling, pussy throbbing over the memory of that morning when he'd bent me over the kitchen counter, gripped my ass, and spread me open so he could lick me from behind. He'd been relentless, bringing me to a shockingly quick orgasm before he'd had to leave, hard as stone, to open the diner.

It turned out I didn't have trouble reaching a climax. I just needed to find the right partner to drown out all the other noise, and Beck had a way of muting every other thought but him.

He leaned forward, his lips brushing against my ear. "Remembering my tongue inside you, baby?"

"Yes," I breathed.

"Are you wet for me?"

"Yes."

"Then what are you waiting for?" he asked, his eyes hot as he stared at me. "If you want my cock, take it out and put it where it belongs. Right inside that perfect pussy."

Never in a million years did I think I would be the kind of person who would be turned on by this—being outside, in the vast open space, the possibility of getting caught nipping at our heels. But I couldn't deny the tightness of my nipples, the wetness gathering in my core, both of which only grew more pronounced with each word from his lips, with each shift of his hips against me, with each caress of his hands on my bare back.

"What if someone walks by?" I asked, breathless, equal parts desperate to hear reassurances as much as I was for him to remind me how easily we could be caught.

Beck's mouth kicked up at the side. "Don't think I didn't notice how you ground that needy pussy on me when you asked that question." He kissed along my jaw, scraping his teeth against the column of my neck before nipping on my earlobe, his lips against the shell of my ear. "Does that turn you on, baby? The thought of someone coming up and seeing how hard you make me? How good I serve this pussy? That you drive me so fucking wild, I can't wait to get you inside before I fuck your sweet cunt?"

My pussy clenched in response to his whispered words, my body aching to be filled by him in a way that I'd never known before Beck.

"Yes," I breathed, reaching down and grappling with the fly of his jeans and his boxer briefs until he sprang free. I wrapped my hand around his thick length, already so hard for me, and pumped him slowly, swiping my thumb through the wetness at his tip.

"Quit teasing," he said through gritted teeth. He slid his hands beneath the hem of my skirt, cupping my ass. "You've had me hard all fucking day. Now, tug those tiny panties aside and give me that hot little pussy."

I shuddered, my body wet and ready for him, already primed for detonation. Sitting up on my knees, I glanced around at the empty swath of land surrounding us as I shifted my panties to the side and slipped his tip inside me. I gasped as he entered me, at the same time my gaze locked on a couple who'd just come around the curve in the road.

I groaned, my pussy clenching around him as I sank down, taking him fully inside me, even as the couple came closer with every step. My clit throbbed, my entire body eager and begging for release.

"Fuck, sunshine. You see them?" he asked, his hands on my ass encouraging me to circle my hips so my clit ground against the base of his cock with every rotation.

"Yes," I breathed, shivers racking my body as my eyes stayed locked on the people getting closer every second, my nipples tight and needy, so desperate for Beck's mouth.

"Christ, you're throbbing. That greedy pussy keeps trying to suck me in deeper, even when you've got every single inch inside you. You love this, don't you? Love knowing you've got a cock fucking you beneath this pretty skirt, looking for all the world like a perfect angel. But you and I both know how dirty my angel can get, don't we? We're the only ones who know your cunt is swallowing me whole. Know that as soon as you come all over my cock, I'm going to explode inside you. And we'll be the only ones who know it's my come dripping down your thighs when you walk by them with a smile."

That was all it took. With the next grind of my clit against him, I shattered. But Beck, as usual, had known it was coming. With one hand still clutching my ass and holding me against him, he cupped the back of my head with the other, tugging my face to his as he swallowed my moans with a kiss. His tongue delved into my mouth, sweeping against my own as his cock jerked, spilling inside me.

He held me against him for long moments, our once-frantic movements now slow and relaxed, his kisses reverent and sweet. Finally, he kissed me twice, then pulled back, the couple who'd witnessed everything without a clue now long gone.

"How was it?" he asked. "Did it live up to the original Chapter Twelve?"

I breathed out a laugh and ran my fingers through his hair. "More than. I love that you do this with me, you know."

"Well, I love you, so we're even."

"I love you, too. So much. You think we'll still be recreating book scenes in five years?"

"I think we're going to be recreating them for the rest of our lives."

I bit my lip, trying to tamp down a smile, my heart cartwheeling in my chest. "The rest of our lives is a pretty long time. Are you sure you're ready for that?"

He brushed my hair back and cupped my face, sweeping his thumbs along my skin. "Sunshine, it could be a hundred years, and it still wouldn't be long enough."

EPILOGUE
BECK

EVERLY ALWAYS RADIATED SUNSHINE, but it practically poured out of her now. *Had been* pouring out of her every second since our talk following the auction. She was perched on my lap as we sat at a table in One Night Stan's—the local bar—while my siblings and dozens of residents surrounded us for a celebration I hadn't allowed myself to even hope for. But today, I could. Because today, they broke ground on our forever home and Starlight Cove's future animal clinic.

We hadn't needed long to finalize everything—Everly had been happy with the plans I'd had drawn up, and Addison had done her Addison thing, becoming a swirling vortex in two seconds flat and whipping everyone into shape so this would be completed sooner rather than later. She'd claimed it was so there was minimal construction on the resort property, but we all knew it was because she loved barking orders.

Until it was finished, Everly and Chuckanut were staying in my apartment, just where I wanted them, and Everly was making house calls to service her clients, while still referring out any surgical procedures to the next closest clinic.

Thankfully, she'd found her rhythm with the house calls—and with Starlight Cove. The former had gotten easier once she'd settled in and figured out the new timing for each appointment. As for the latter... Well, after Mabel's video in which Everly could see firsthand just how much everyone in town loved her, it'd become easier for her to see it for herself.

Brady sat next to me, Luna's position mirroring Everly's as she sat on his lap. Smiling at Addison, Luna leaned forward, bracing her arms on the table while Brady curled a possessive hand around her hip.

"I'm telling you, with your spa offerings, it's going to be *gold*. And I think I can really sell Harper on that article idea," Addison said, hands flying as she spoke, narrowly missing toppling over several glasses in her wake. "Weddings could be our next big draw!" Her words were a little sloppy, eyes a little glazed.

I glanced over at Aiden and raised a brow, silently telling him he'd better make sure she got back to the inn safely when she was ready to leave. He just tipped his chin at me, already on it. Thank God, because I didn't plan to be here. I was already itching to get home and out of the crowd. Lose myself in Everly for a while.

Or all night.

Levi downed the last of his drink before setting it on the table with a clunk. He'd shown up, scowl firmly on his face, and slid into a chair without a word, only offering Everly and me a nod of congratulations, though that'd been more than I was expecting. To be honest, I was surprised he'd come at all.

With a groan, Levi said, "This is why I never hang out with you. Can you talk about literally anything else but the resort? Do you even have a life?"

"Oh, that's rich coming from Starlight Cove's hermit," Addison shot back with an eye roll.

"What are you, twelve?" Aiden said to them both. "Christ, I'm having flashbacks to when you were little and constantly fighting."

"I kind of like it," Everly said with a shrug. "Reminds me of me and my brother."

"I wish we could've officially met him," Luna said. "Does he have any plans to visit again?"

Everly took a sip of her fruity cocktail and nodded. "Definitely after the house is built. He and my parents are excited to see it."

"We all are," Addison said. Then she snapped her fingers and narrowed one eye in a move that made her look like a pirate. "That reminds me...I need to talk to Ford about adding flower boxes to the cottages. Where is he?"

She twisted around, looking for my twin and nearly falling out of her chair while she was at it. Fucking hell, Aiden was going to have to drag her out like a sack of potatoes.

"He's around here somewhere," I said, glancing around and finding him standing in the corner with Quinn, the two of them facing off in some kind of heated exchange. Par for the course with them.

As the rest of the table continued chatting and exchanging barbs, I turned my attention back to Everly. "How is Brother Dick Breath doing anyway?"

She huffed out a laugh and twisted on my lap, effectively rubbing her tight ass against my cock and making me swallow back a groan. We'd overslept this morning, which meant I hadn't had my daily fix of her pussy yet, and I was dying for it.

"Are you two *ever* going to get along?" she asked.

I shrugged, one hand palming her ass, the other resting on her bare knee, my thumb slipping beneath the fluttery hem of her short skirt. "That depends on if he plans to be an absolute shitstain the next time he visits or not."

"Do you just have, like, a thesaurus of insults for him that you run through, or what?"

"It's easy when I have the right inspiration."

She rolled her eyes, but a grin tugged at her lips. "What do I have to do so you'll be nice to him?"

I *should* be nice to him. He was her brother, after all, and my initial impression of him couldn't have been more off. And he did look out for her, even if it was in his own misguided way. But it was going to take a hell of a lot for that first impression—not to mention his efforts to try to drag her back to Washington—to fade.

"Oh, it'd have to be good, for sure," I said.

She draped her arms over my shoulders, playing with the hair peeking out from under my hat. "How about you choose our next chapter?"

My brows lifted. Everly usually steered that ship, and I was all too willing to let her be the captain. There was little else in this world I loved more than pleasing her, and finding all her pleasure buttons was a quest I would gladly pursue for the rest of my life. But I couldn't deny a few chapters recently had piqued my interest when she hadn't said much at all about them.

"How long do I have to be nice to him for?"

She tossed her head back and laughed, the tinkling noise heard even over the chorus of voices in the bar. I fucking loved that sound. Loved knowing I'd been the one to make her laugh. Loved knowing I made her happy, period.

When she stared back at me, her eyes were shining, so full of love and contentment, it nearly had me in a choke hold. Christ, this woman was my whole fucking world, and all I could do was orbit around her. She'd come into my life, not like a hurricane but like the rising sun, her warmth seeping over me, her sunshine illuminating all my dark shadows.

I never wanted to spend a day without her sparkle.

And I was going to spend the rest of my life making sure I didn't have to.

I leaned in and brushed my lips against her ear. "When can we leave? I haven't been inside you since last night, and that's too fucking long. I'm going through withdrawals."

She shook her head, a look of mock disapproval on her face. "You're insatiable." Then she leaned in and tugged on my lower lip with her teeth. "But soon."

Before I could stand with her in my lap and carry her out, fuck what anyone else thought, Ford and Quinn walked closer, their body language radiating tension.

"That's not how it happened, and you know it," he said.

Quinn's voice was dry when she replied, "What I know is this was all your idea."

"Oh, you *wish* it was my idea. Have you already forgotten?"

"Forgotten how much you begged for it?" Quinn scoffed. "Not hardly."

"Tell yourself whatever you need to, Doc, but I know the truth."

"All you know are your delusions." With that, Quinn stalked out the door without a backward glance, and Ford stood next to our table, jaw set, looking torn between going after her or downing a bottle of tequila.

In the end, he turned to the bartender—a new transplant to Starlight Cove—and tapped on the bar top. "Tequila. And make it a double."

The bartender's brows lifted as he poured Ford the drink. "Trouble with an ex?"

Ford huffed out a laugh, shaking his head and mumbling something under his breath that sounded an awful lot like, *I wish.* Then he downed half his drink at once and said, "Actually, she's about to be my wife."

OTHER TITLES BY BRIGHTON WALSH

ABOUT THE AUTHOR

Award-winning *USA Today* and *Wall Street Journal* bestselling author Brighton Walsh spent a decade as a professional photographer before taking her storytelling in a different direction and reconnecting with her first love—writing. She likes her books how she likes her tea —steamy and satisfying—and adores strong-willed heroines and the protective heroes who fall head over heels for them. Brighton lives in the Midwest with her real life hero of a husband, her two kids—both taller than her—and her dog who thinks she's a queen. Her boy-filled house is the setting for dirty socks galore, frequent dance parties (okay, so it's mostly her, by herself, while her children look on in horror), and more laughter than she thought possible.

www.brightonwalsh.com

tiktok.com/@brightonwalshbooks
instagram.com/brighton_walsh
facebook.com/brightonwalshwrites
twitter.com/brightonwalsh

Printed in Great Britain
by Amazon